THE PIPER'S LADY

THE MACLARENS (BOOK THREE)

SHERRY EWING

Kingsburg Pres
P.O. Box 475146
San Francisco, CA 94147
www.kingsburgpress.com

The Piper's Lady is a work of fiction. Names, characters, places, and incidents are a product of the author's imagination. Locales and public names are sometimes used for atmospheric purposes. Any resemblance to actual people, living or dead, or to businesses, companies, events, institutions, or locales is completely coincidental.

Editor: Jude Knight
Cover Design: Sherry Ewing

Cover Couple Photo: The Kiss by Francesco Hayez (1791–1882)
Cover Background: View of Tantallon Castle by Alexander Nasmyth (1758–1840)

The Piper's Lady/Sherry Ewing -- 2nd ed.
ISBN eBook: 978-1-946177-55-1
ISBN Print: 978-1-946177-56-8
Library of Congress Control Number: 2020917760

OTHER BOOKS BY SHERRY EWING

Medieval & Time Travel Series

To Love A Scottish Laird: *De Wolfe Pack Connected World*

To Love An English Knight: *De Wolfe Pack Connected World*

If My Heart Could See You: *The MacLarens (Book One)*

For All of Ever: The Knights of Berwyck, A Quest Through Time (Book One)

Only For You: The Knights of Berwyck, A Quest Through Time (Book Two)

Hearts Across Time: The Knights of Berwyck, A Quest Through Time (Books One & Two)

A special box set of For All of Ever & Only For You

A Knight To Call My Own: *The MacLarens (Book Two)*

To Follow My Heart: The Knights of Berwyck, A Quest Through Time (Book Three)

The Piper's Lady: *The MacLarens (Book Three)*

Love Will Find You: The Knights of Berwyck, A Quest Through Time (Book Four)

One Last Kiss: The Knights of Berwyck,

A Quest Through Time (Book Five)

Regency

A Kiss for Charity: *A de Courtenay Novella (Book One)*

The Earl Takes A Wife: *A de Courtenay Novella (Book Two)*

Nothing But Time, *A Family of Worth: Book One*

One Moment In Time: *A Family of Worth, Book Two*

Under the Mistletoe

A Second Chance At Love in ***Fire & Frost:*** *A Bluestocking Belles Collection*

Learn more about Sherry's books on her website at www.SherryEwing.com/books

Join Sherry's newsletter at http://bit.ly/2vGrqQM

THE PIPER'S LADY

For my dear friend Melissa.

Distance may keep us apart but you are always close to my heart. I love you, sis!

CHAPTER 1

Château d'Usson, France
Winter, the Year of Our Lord's Grace 1181

The raspy breathing of the man lying prone upon the bed filled the chamber. Death had been hovering close at hand, ready to claim another soul, and yet still he clung onto life. Even the blizzard outside the chateau's walls hinted at how little time he had left.

Coira Norwood sat at her mending near the hearth. For months, she had watched her once vibrant grandfather dwindle into a frail old man. 'Twas hard to observe the knight who had raised her come to such a fate. She had followed him for years to wherever their paths would lead. True, he had told her on more than one occasion 'twas well past time she should wed instead. Still, she could not bear to leave his side, not when he had done so much for her. She had resolved to stay as his companion for however long he graced this earth. Time was no longer on his side.

The door to her grandfather's bedchamber unexpectedly opened. Flakes of the flurry pelting the outside world clung to the dark red mantle of the knight who entered. He shook the rest of the snow from his thick, shoulder-length mane of black hair before discarding his cloak and draping it over his arm. Morgan, lately of Berwyck, was like another brother to Coira. He had known her since she was a small child, when she had followed behind him and her older brother, Rolf, begging for their affection. Yet boys would be boys, and in their youth, they had teased her relentlessly. Setting aside such childish spats, she had long since forgiven them both, although she had not seen Morgan for many a year.

"Morgan," she exclaimed, keeping her voice hushed so she did not wake her grandfather. "This is such an unexpected surprise. Welcome!"

"'Tis good to see you, Coira," he replied, with a smile she remembered from their youth together.

She took his mantle, tossing the garment on a nearby chair, before grasping his chilled hands. "You are freezing, Morgan. Come, sit by the fire and warm yourself." He leaned down to fondly kiss both her cheeks and followed her to the hearth.

"'Tis good to at last locate you, Coira," he declared, holding out his hands towards the flames.

"You have traveled far to find us, I see."

"Aye. It has been a difficult journey riddled with misfortune. 'Tis almost a miracle of God I have found you at all."

She waited for him to tell her more, although her heart already sensed the heavy weight of whatever news he carried. One did not travel all the way from England and the whole length of France in the dead of winter to bear tidings of joy.

"I should see to having a meal prepared for you. You must be famished." She ran her shaking hands down the length of her gown as she jumped up to see about his meal. But Morgan had other plans. He halted her progress to the door by grabbing her wrist.

"That is not of import right now, Coira." He hesitated and nodded towards the bed. "How is he?"

She followed his gaze and shook her head. "Stubborn as always and wishing to be home instead of abusing the good graces of a distant cousin. He has been ill for a while now. I have been afraid to have him travel in his current condition. Considering how long it would take to reach home now that winter has set in, I am not certain he would survive the journey. To be honest, I am surprised he has lasted this long."

Morgan gave a heavy sigh. "Then I fear the news I bear will not do you, nor him, any good. I was tasked to find you almost a year ago but met every possible obstacle on my way. I did not expect you to be traveling this far south and had just about given up hope of ever reaching you."

"Aye, we are a long way from home, Morgan. My grandfather seemed to be on a sort of pilgrimage… his words, not mine. He wished to see all the places of his youth before he departed this earth. I could hardly let him travel so far without me."

He gave a small smile. "That sounds just as I remember him. I have always admired the man's youthful stamina."

Coira gave a quiet chuckle. "You should tell him so. 'Twill bring him joy to hear such words from someone he cares so much about. But you did not come all this way for idle conversation. What is your news? Is it Rolf? What has my handsome brother been up to near the wilds of Scotland?" Her teasing manner was forced. Better to make light of the situation whilst she could, for her heart whispered she would not like where this conversation would eventually lead.

Movement upon the bed had them both waiting to see if her grandfather had awoken.

"Coira, who… is here with you, child?" her grandfather forced out. They went to the bedside. Morgan helped the fragile man to a sitting position. "Morgan… dear boy—" he began before coughing stole his breath. After several minutes he was at last able to speak. "Are you really here with us, or are you but a figment of my imagination?"

"Grandfather, he is hardly a boy any longer, just as I

am no longer a mere child," Coira muttered, embarrassment flushing her face. At the age of a score and ten, her youth was long past.

"Aye. I am here on a most serious matter," Morgan replied, taking hold of the man's hand before turning his gaze upon Coira. "Sir Walter has earned the right to call me anything he so wishes, is this not so, sir?"

Grandfather squeezed each of their hands before closing his eyes. A tear slid down his cheek. "I was dreaming… of Rolf. It has been so long since I have seen him. In my dreams, he gives this old man comfort, telling me stories of his exploits with the Devil's Dragon of Blackmore."

"Lord Dristan is now at Berwyck, Sir Walter, and has resided there for many a year. He is married with two children now."

"Married? I can hardly believe such drivel," Grandfather declared, as though his strength returned to him with the mere mention of Rolf's liege lord. "The Devil's Dragon? Settled? Surely you jest with me."

"I would not dare, sir," Morgan replied, hiding a smirk.

The old man's eyes opened. "And Rolf?"

Coira gazed upon Morgan and watched his face fall. She knew what his next words would be. "'Tis why you are here, is it not? To give us word about my brother?"

"Aye, but 'tis not news you will wish to hear."

"No! Do not tell me my brother is gone from this world, I beg of you," she cried out.

"More than anything, I wish I could give you news he yet lives, but he has perished. I am sorry I was not able to let you know of his demise sooner."

"Did he... die... in battle?" Sir Walter choked out, with a sob.

"Aye. No knight could ask for a more noble or honorable death. He was saving Lord Dristan's sister-in-law, the Lady Lynet. His sacrifice allowed her to get away with another who was sent to rescue her."

Coira collapsed into Morgan's arms, sobbing. His arms enveloped her, and she felt his hand brushing her hair to offer her comfort. "No! Tell me you but speak a falsehood."

He kissed the top of her head. "I am most sorry, little one. You know Rolf was like a brother to me, as well. I miss him dearly."

Her grandfather's coughing had Coira rising and rushing to the hearth where she kept broth warm to sooth his parched throat when he was in need. She helped him sip the brew before he fell back onto the pillows. Exhaustion and pain marred his face.

"Where is he buried?" her grandfather asked, when he could speak again. Coira sat on the edge of his bed, numb.

"At Berwyck Castle, Sir Walter. He rests in a place of honor within the family cemetery. The Lady Lynet cared for your son very much, as did all those who resided within the castle walls.

"Morgan, I must ask a favor of you."

"I am yours to command," Morgan answered with a nod.

Her grandfather reached out for her hand and joined it with Morgan's. "I must ask you to… to take care of my granddaughter. She must wed—"

"Grandfather! I cannot marry Morgan. He is like a brother to me," Coira blurted out in shock. "Besides… look at me. I am far too old for any man to want to marry me. And too plain! Who would want to look at this face for the rest of his life?"

"Stop that!" her grandfather bellowed with far more strength than she would have thought possible. "First and foremost, you are a beautiful woman in any man's eyes if they but care to look deep enough. You would do a knight proud as their wife."

"But Grandfather, Morg—"

"Second… do not interrupt your elders, missy," he teased with blue twinkling eyes. "I am not asking Morgan to wed you, although heaven knows he would be blessed if you took him for your husband."

Morgan breathed a sigh of relief, and Coira raised her brow at him. "No offense, Coira. You know I love you, but only as a sister."

Grandfather cleared his throat. "May I finish, children?" At their nod, he continued. "Take her to Berwyck with you, my boy, and see to it you and her cousin Lord Dristan find someone to love her for who she is. I will give you monies to see to her comfort, but I do not wish to pass from this world without knowing she is taken care of by someone who cares for her."

"I cannot leave you, Grandfather. You need me," Coira protested, leaning in to give the man a hug. He gave her an affectionate pat upon her back.

She sat up, and he cupped her face with his hands. "You have been such a blessing in my life, dear sweet Coira, but 'tis time for you to spread your wings and fly. You have done your duty by watching over me all these years, and no grandfather has ever been prouder to have his darling granddaughter by his side. I have been selfish, keeping you with me for so long. You should have wed and had children of your own by now."

"I did not mind. You know how much I love you," she murmured.

"And I love you as well. Go to Berwyck. Say a prayer at Rolf's grave for me and live your life. You have done your duty to me, child. Now 'tis time for you to find someone of your own to love and call your husband." He turned his gaze upon Morgan. "You will take care of her for me?" he asked with pleading eyes.

"Aye, sir. I will treat her with all the respect I have always held for her… as a beloved sister."

"'Tis good, then. Now, Coira, leave us so I can discuss arrangements with this young man and hear about his travels. And perchance, I will live one more adventure through his eyes."

Coira left the bedchamber to seek out a servant to

send a meal up to Morgan. Emotionally drained, she then went to her own room where she could mourn the loss of her beloved brother. She could still hardly believe he was gone.

Several more months passed before Morgan and Coira were at last able to begin their travels to Berwyck Castle. With a final farewell to the chateau she had called home and spring finally in the air, she rose from her grandfather's gravesite. Morgan had assured her he would see the property her grandfather had left her was secured, and yet she was still uncertain that any would willingly wed her, given her age. The thought of the other life for a single woman—as a nun—made her shudder. Entering a convent to devote her life to God was not for her. Quaking at the thought, she lifted her chin and took her first steps towards her new future.

CHAPTER 2

Berwyck Castle, near Scotland's Border
Summer, the Year of our Lord's Grace 1182

The mournful sound of a bagpipe filled the early hours of the day. Deep baritone voices of the garrison knights shouted as they practiced their maneuvers in perfect unison. Feet stomped and chainmail clinked whilst the men pounded their swords upon their shields before raising them over their heads or in front of them, depending on their position. They quickly formed into a tight formation as though they were protecting themselves from arrows flying through the air.

Piper Garrick of Clan MacLaren maintained the steady rhythm of his instrument, keeping the army at its paces upon the lists. How they managed to drill so relentlessly for hours upon hours was beyond him, although he knew that any complaints would merely serve to anger their liege lord. Garrick was only too happy to keep to his task instead of joining the men at their training. He knew just how physically brutal such training tactics could be.

"Cease, Garrick," Laird Dristan shouted as he passed, whilst raising his hand to halt his men. The final notes of Garrick's bagpipe faded in the morning air.

Dristan strode across the field towards his knights, then called out, "'Tis passable, although I expected you to sharpen those moves at least an hour ago."

As he listened to his laird chastising his knights, relief flooded Garrick, knowing his part of the day's exercises was at an end. As he began to leave the lists, someone bellowed out his name. Flinching, Garrick turned, dreading what would still be required of him this day.

"Where go you, Piper?" Dristan shouted, with a laugh. "The day is yet young!"

"What would ye like me tae play next, my laird?" Garrick asked, raising the pipe to his lips and wondering what his laird would order the knights to practice next.

"Play? Your playing is over for the day. Pick up your sword and let us see how you have improved. Your life may depend upon your skill with the blade in the heat of battle."

"My instrument will serve me just as well in such a

moment, my laird," he called back. Thrusting out his pipes, he jabbed at the air as though to disarm an unseen enemy before him. Amused guffaws heckled him. Garrick frowned. He hated when the men assumed he was incapable of protecting himself.

"By all that is holy, our piper would not last a minute with those moves," a knight named Cederick called out.

Turquine and Teagan, two knights who loved to instigate trouble, burst out chuckling in complete unison before Turquine bellowed, "Shall we have a wager, men?"

Another knight, Nathaniel, joined in the merriment. "'Twould not be much of a bet when those pipes snap in two with his first efforts."

Finlay, of Lady Amiria's personal guard, stepped forward. "I shall take yer bet and double the wager in Garrick's favor," he proclaimed, pulling out several coins from a pouch hanging from his belt.

Garrick nodded to his clansman, pleased with the man's faith in him.

"Aye," chimed in Dougal, another of Amiria's guardsmen. Dougal began pushing aside one knight after another till he was standing at the front of the men. "No man of the MacLaren clan would lose so easily. I shall even take Garrick's place on the off chance he fails in his quest to win," he added, nodding to Garrick across the field. "No offense, Piper."

Garrick smirked. "None taken, Dougal, but there

shall be no need tae replace me. I am more than capable of holding my own against any one of these guardsmen."

Drake, one of the biggest knights on the lists, stepped forward, looking him over. "Keep your coins. Any fool can see for himself Garrick would lose such a battle."

Garrick motioned with his hand. "Do ye think so? Then, come and try tae knock me off me feet," he jeered, even whilst the knights ignored Drake's words and began wagering amongst themselves.

Drake cracked his knuckles and smirked. "'Twill be my pleasure, Piper, to put you in your place. I will even give you the advantage and not use my sword to disarm you."

Bertram, the captain of Dristan's personal guard, stepped forward and shouted out. "Best watch your words, Drake, for you might regret them when you land on your sorry arse!" Loud guffaws rang out in the lists.

Garrick hid a smirk of satisfaction and spread his feet into position. His confidence grew as he recalled the training Bertram had drilled into him in the quiet hours of the eve whilst everyone else ate and drank their fill.

Drake slipped the belt from his waist and let his sword fall to the ground. "I do not think so. What does a mere piper know about swordplay or staying alive in the middle of a battle?"

"My coinage is on our piper," Dristan stated, causing several knights to pause whilst placing their wager with Turquine. Their laird dismounted from his horse and came to stand on the edge of the lists with arms folded across his chest. "Show them and Drake a thing or two, Garrick."

Knowing Laird Dristan had faith in his abilities caused Garrick's pride to rise. As Drake approached, Garrick looked for any signs of an opening where he could thrust his pipe without causing the instrument damage. But the knight before him had not earned his place as one of Laird Dristan's personal guardsmen by being an inferior fighter. Nay. This knight would show him no mercy in his quest to prove Garrick did not belong on the field.

Drake stood before him a moment, eyeing his adversary. Then, he made a sudden move, causing Garrick to jump back.

Drake laughed and turned his head back towards the men. "You see?" he mocked. "His place is here at the castle with the women and ch—"

The air rushed out of Drake with a loud whoosh as Garrick thrust his pipes into his adversary's neck. Garrick had had but an instant to react when Drake foolishly turned his attention elsewhere in his cockiness and he had taken the chance so readily presented to him. Tossing his bagpipes aside, Garrick jabbed at Drake's midsection with his shoulder, and then dropped to the ground as Drake took a wild swing at him. With Drake off balance, Garrick quickly rolled into the man's legs, causing the knight to fall over. Just as fast, Garrick jumped on top of the fallen knight and pulled out his dirk, placing his weapon at the man's neck.

Everything had happened so quickly, Berwyck's knights could only gape at their piper. Moans from those who had wagered on the wrong man filled the air as the men began exchanging coins.

Laird Dristan clapped his hands and nodded approval at his captain, Bertram. Clearly, the two were in cahoots. "Well done, Garrick! Well done," Dristan beamed, before turning his attention to his men. "Never underestimate your opponent."

Garrick replaced his blade and stood, offering a hand to Drake. The knight stared upon the proffered limb as though he had thoughts of severing Garrick's hand from his arm. Finally, with a self-effacing chuckle, Drake accepted Garrick's offer to help him stand.

"By damn, 'twas indeed well done, Garrick," Drake conceded, slapping him upon his back.

"Never let it be said a MacLaren does not know how tae improvise or use whatever means necessary tae take the advantage," Garrick boasted, with a smile of satisfaction.

The two men clasped arms before Drake bent over to pick up the discarded bagpipes and handed them to Garrick. "I will remember to listen to the words of

Lord Dristan. Since he put his wager on you, I should have known I was destined to fail. I will not make the same mistake again."

Dristan stepped forward. "Shall we get back to our training, men? We are burning daylight, though this exercise is a good lesson to show you all need as much training as I can pound into your thick heads." Another groan filled the air before all turned to take up their swords and battle axes. "Drake, you have the privilege of continuing to train with Garrick. Show him what you can do with a blade and ensure he is just as capable as the rest of the men... yourself included."

"Aye, my lord," Drake answered with a wicked smirk. Pulling his sword from his scabbard, he tested the blade by swinging the weapon in the air. "Let us be about it, Piper. As our liege lord has said, we are wasting daylight."

Garrick took up his own sword knowing the rest of the afternoon would be long, and he would soon pay the price for his one moment of glory.

CHAPTER 3

Coira stared at the fortress set high upon a cliff near the ocean's shore. No enemy in their right mind would ever dare attempt to penetrate such a formidable structure, much less succeed. And yet, from the stories Morgan had told her during their travels, 'twas exactly what the Devil's Dragon had accomplished many years ago in the name of his king. The fact that Morgan and Rolf were amongst the men who had dared such a feat left Coria dumbstruck.

She had never been close to her cousin and knew little of the man Dristan had become, although Rolf had always said he was honored to serve as his vassal. She knew most of what was said about Dristan of Berwyck was a falsehood. Rumors had reached her as far away as the south of France about her cousin's ruthlessness upon the battlefield, and some hinted that his dragonish nature extended to his domestic life. His skill with a sword was how he had become a champion knight for King Henry II, but he was also married and a father, and both Rolf and Morgan admired him. Surely he would find a place within his household for her? She hated the thought of having to join a nunnery. Still... Dristan's reputation might be a forewarning of what she could expect. 'Twas no small wonder her stomach was tied up in nervous knots, for she was unsure of the welcome she would receive at Berwyck.

Horse and riders both seemed eager to finally be at their journey's end, and they made quick work of lessening the distance to the castle. Coira would be relieved to rest her head upon something softer than the ground and feel something more stable than a rolling ship beneath her feet. After her grandfather's long final illness, she had become unused the rigors of travel.

'Twas not long before they were riding through the barbican gate and beneath the deadly portcullis. Nor was it long before lads came to relieve them of the steeds who had carried them to the safety of the keep. With Morgan's help, Coira dismounted from her horse, and she all but fell against him as her knees buckled beneath her.

Morgan chuckled. "Easy now, Coira. I have you."

She rested her forehead against his chest whilst he steadied her. "I am most sorry, Morgan," she mumbled her apology. "Give me just a moment to find my legs."

"But of course, my dear," he said keeping his arms

around her for support. "Perchance you could take your ease on the bench over yonder beneath that tree whilst I find someone to escort you to a room. Then, I will inform Lord Dristan you have arrived."

She lifted her head to stare over at the bench but had no desire to spend more of her time sitting. "Nay, do not yet leave me amongst these strangers," she replied softly, feeling oddly vulnerable. This was the first time she had ventured so far from her grandfather in many a year.

He laughed, tipping up her chin to assess her face, which surely must have showed all her emotions bubbling up to the surface. "Where is the young woman I knew so long ago? She was made of much sterner stuff than to let a new adventure get the best of her."

"'Twas all a façade, I assure you," she grumbled.

"I think you voice a falsehood, but let it not be said I left a fair damsel in distress to fend for herself." He tucked her hand into the crook of his elbow. "Let us go see firsthand how my liege lord trains his knights, for they will be practicing upon the lists at this hour of the day. You shall be most impressed with your cousin's efforts to ensure Berwyck's safety."

Coira followed him, taking in her surroundings as they made their way through the grounds. Berwyck Castle was a thriving community. How many people lived and worked here? Serfs and servants ran to and fro on some errand or another, all to the sound of the steady beat of the blacksmith's hammer upon an anvil. But the everyday noise of a thriving castle was nothing compared to the sound of the men who trained for war, their voices ringing in the air.

As the lists came into view, Coira all but stopped her progress at Morgan's side. 'Twas a remarkable sight, and she could almost envision her brother amongst these men training beside them. A sob tore at her heart, but she refused to let Morgan see her grief, nor the fear that arose from being alone in the world and dependent on the kindness of strangers.

Morgan led her over to a lone stone bench. Once seated, he kissed her hand. "You can watch from here whilst I report to my lord. I shall not be long."

Without waiting for her reply, he began making his way to the field and she fidgeted on the hard stone bench beneath her sore backside. Her attempts to get comfortable failed and she stood, clenching her hands at her side so she did not do something so unladylike as to actually rub her bruised bottom after their long journey. She refused to make a spectacle of herself on her first moments at her new home.

Her eyes swept over those who jousted in the distance and to the men who were closer, practicing with their swords. One in particular drew her attention, and she held her breath when she witnessed him narrowly missing the blade aimed at his head. He all but laughed at his opponent as though daring him to take another swipe at him. The other knight obliged him with a swing of his sword and a chuckle of his own. She continued to view the first knight's performance as though he was the center of attention, like a bard entertaining a hall's inhabitants. Her eyes were fixated on him, and he held her captivated with his display and prowess with his weapon of war.

This warrior knight was magnificent. Coira could not remember any other man who had made her heart beat so furiously in her chest with just one look. Tawny colored hair was tossed from his exertion and the faint ocean breeze. Muscles bulged on his arm as he hefted his sword again and again. She could not take her eyes from him, and then something she had waited for her whole life happened. 'Twas as though some unseen force slammed into her, causing her to lose her breath.

Their eyes met across the distance of the field, and 'twas if there was no space between them at all. The sounds from the lists, so vibrant just moments before, faded into nothingness whilst they were focused, one to the other. His sword dropped useless from his hand. A name was called but was lost to her as he instinctively ducked to miss a blow from the other knight. Yet he continued to gaze only upon her. An instant seemed like an eternity, and Coira was lost in a moment that would surely be ingrained into her memory for the rest of her life.

As she continued to observe him, his eyes widened in what seemed like concern, and he began running towards her.

"Coira!"

Someone shouted her name, the bellow louder than the noise of the men practicing in the field, bringing her quickly back to reality. Alarm raced through her as she realized she had somehow wandered onto the field. Two knights were so focused upon their training, they did not see her, and Coira feared for her life when a sword was ripped from one of the knight's hands and sailed through the air in her direction.

Arms of steel wrapped around her and she was flung to the ground, air rushing from her lungs. The knight who had saved her tightened his arms around her when he rolled so he bore the brunt of the impact. Her cheek pressed firmly to his chest, she heard the frantic beating of his heart, and she knew without any doubt exactly who was holding her before she even looked up to see his face.

Coira held tighter to the knight beneath her, no matter how inappropriate her current position was to those witnessing the scene. But she cared not and could not move even if 'twould save her life yet again. Unbeknownst to the knight whose name she did not yet know, she was certain of their instant connection. She would hold onto this moment whilst she could for she did not doubt she must be dreaming.

CHAPTER 4

Garrick gasped in relief upon seeing the woman he held securely in his arms had come to no harm. 'Twas a close call. She lifted her head from his chest. Hazel eyes stared back at him in bewilderment. He searched her face. Hers was not a classical beauty, and yet Garrick had the distinct impression this woman had a beautiful soul. Where such a thought came from, he knew not. Who was she?

"You saved me," she whispered in a shaky tone. "You are truly a gallant knight to rescue me. Your liege lord must value you as one of his warriors."

Warrior? Him? He opened his mouth to correct her assumption but could not find the words. She would think less of him if she knew he was only the clan's piper.

"Are ye harmed?" he murmured, still holding the pleasing womanly curves of the lady who had not yet moved from atop him. Her brow rose, and Garrick inwardly cursed knowing there was no way to hide his Scottish accent.

"Nay, but only because of your ability to move so quickly. Thank you, Sir…" She left her sentence linger in the air between them.

"Garrick," he answered, giving her his name, "of Clan MacLaren."

"My thanks, Sir Garrick," she replied with a kind smile.

The lists had become eerily silent, with the exception of one person running in their direction.

"Get your hands off her!" a voice bellowed.

Before either of them could move, the woman was ripped from his arms, and Garrick saw her enveloped in the fierce embrace of Morgan. She wrapped her arms around his neck, and jealousy assaulted Garrick's emotions and tugged at his heartstrings.

"Coira! By St. Michael's Wings you gave me such a fright, woman," Morgan scolded in concern. Setting her down upon her feet, he proceeded to clasp both her cheeks before placing kisses on each.

"There is no need to fuss, Morgan, I am fine."

"Fine? You just about had your head severed from your neck! What the bloody hell were you doing walking through the training field?" Morgan berated whilst he continued assessing her for any injuries.

Garrick watched the woman Morgan called Coira shrug before she turned and leveled a bright smile upon him. "As you can plainly see for yourself, this brave knight came to my rescue. I have come to no harm only because of his quickness and fleetness of foot. Such a chivalrous warrior!" She turned to Garrick with a slight bow of her head. "I offer you my thanks, Sir Garrick."

A snort escaped Morgan, and with furrowed brows, he gave a sarcastic chuckle. "*Sir* Garrick?"

Before Garrick could once more defend himself, a roar of laughter came from the field as the men listened in on the conversation. Their voices jumbled together as they began placing wagers once again. Garrick scowled at the words "love struck" amongst the bets being made.

Dristan's voice boomed over his men. "Enough! Get back to your training, lest you wish to continue into the late evening hours." He came to stand next to them.

"My laird," Garrick offered a short bow.

"I see you have become acquainted with Lady Coira, Garrick," Dristan said with a nod to the lady, "although 'twas not necessarily how I would have introduced Rolf's sister to those who live within Berwyck's walls."

'Twas Garrick's turn to be stunned. "Rolf's… sister?"

"Aye, and my cousin," Dristan replied, taking the woman's hand and placing it in the crook of his elbow. "She has come to stay with us and will be under my protection."

"My lady," Garrick bowed once again. "'Tis a pleasure tae meet ye."

"The pleasure is mine, Sir Garrick," Coira replied, whilst she watched him intently.

Garrick felt his laird's stare but did not correct the use of a title Garrick had no right to claim.

Dristan cleared his throat. "Well then, since the lady is unharmed, you may go back to your training, Garrick. I am sure Lady Coira is in need of rest after her long journey." He waved to a nearby servant. "Head up to the keep, Lady Coira, where you shall be introduced to my wife. She will see you settled until we can meet later in my solar."

Garrick watched her leave with Morgan, who draped his arm possessively around Coira's waist. God's Blood... she was his laird's cousin and Rolf's sister. Who would have thought a sister of Rolf's could be so lovely?

"Stay away from her, Garrick. You are not good enough for her. She deserves better."

Rolf's voice came inside Garrick's mind, startling him. *Perfect! Now I am going tae have a ghost berating me for ogling his sister,* Garrick mused. He heard Rolf's laughter once again in his head.

"Until the end of your days," the voice said.

He picked his sword up from the ground and began running back to the field with his laird. Mayhap if he trained hard enough, those sudden feelings for Coira would be driven out of his heart. At least he could try...

CHAPTER 5

The solar door swung open and her cousin filled the space with his presence. So many years had passed that Coira had all but forgotten how impressive Dristan had become. But the welcoming smile upon his face set most of her fears to rest.

"Cousin," he said, opening his arms. "It has been far too long since our paths have crossed."

She was enfolded into a fierce hug. "My Lord Dristan," she murmured. "'Tis good to see you. Thank you for receiving me."

"You can cease with any of that title business, Coira. We are family. As such, we need no formalities between us."

"How are your mother and father?" she asked, wishing her own parents yet lived. He took her hand and ushered her to a seat by the fire.

"They are well, the last I heard from them." He went

to pour them a goblet of wine and Coira had the distinct feeling he did not wish to have speech about his parents.

"I pray you do not mind that I am here."

"Mind? Why ever would I mind?"

Coira sipped her wine whilst she watched her cousin take a seat across from her. "Your poor relation coming to beg lodging from her rich cousin does not bother you? Generally this does not sit well with most people."

"You are hardly poor and I am not like most people. If you would take a moment to recall, I sent Morgan to find you. Hence, you are welcome here."

"You are too kind, Dristan," she whispered in relief, taking another sip of her wine.

"I regret the years we have spent apart. We are family after all and I feel responsible for your welfare. I have plans for you and will make it a priority to find you a suitable husband." He grinned as if he had already picked out the man she would wed.

Her wine almost spewed from her lips until she choked on the liquid instead. "A husband?"

"Aye! I have several noblemen in mind who would be adequate to provide a good life for you. I will ensure no one less than a knight presses their suit."

"*Adequate?* Dristan I–"

"No need to thank me. I shall see to all the details and send runners to those whom I think will make a good match." He drained his wine, stood, and came over to her side. Leaning down, he pressed a kiss upon her cheek. "'Tis good to see you, Coira. I will see you at the evening meal."

Dristan left just as quickly as he arrived whilst Coira sat there stunned. A nunnery was looking more appealing than a life spent with some unknown man who would make only an *adequate* husband. However, nothing could be done immediately. She would let the matter rest for now.

~

AFTER SEVERAL DAYS of learning her way around the castle and becoming comfortable with its many passages, Coira was at last able to pay her respects to her brother, although she should have made this a priority when she first arrived. Mayhap 'twas the thought of Rolf lying in a cold grave that kept her from visiting. She looked down upon the headstone, thankful his resting place was a peaceful one in the MacLaren family cemetery. He was buried in a place of honor. She could not ask for more from these pleasant strangers.

Coira placed a small bouquet of flowers at the base of Rolf's headstone before she knelt upon the ground. Making the sign of the cross, she began to pray her brother's soul found peace in the heavens above. Tales of his bravery when rescuing the Lady Lynet had torn at her heart. 'Twas just like Rolf to sacrifice himself in order to save another. She would have expected no less from her brother for whom she had the highest regard. He had always seemed larger than life and mayhap she should not have held him to such high esteem. Yet, how could she not? Rolf could never do wrong in her eyes, unless 'twas to tease her in their youth.

Rather than staying true to her prayers, her mind wandered. She remembered their childhood and the few times he had returned to visit her as she grew older. Though such occasions had been scarce, the years had always seemed to melt away with his appearance. Tears flowed down her cheeks at the thought of her brother dying alone somewhere north in the wilds of Scotland.

She glanced up, imagining she could sense his presence. "Rolf?" she whispered to the wind.

There was no answer, nor was there any sight of his ghostly form guarding her. Perchance those who had spoken of seeing him at Berwyck were but playing a cruel joke upon her. 'Twas not right someone would take advantage of her grief, but how else could she explain those who told her Rolf wandered Berwyck's halls? Such tales gave her the smallest increment of hope he was somehow near, watching her. However, if he did indeed stand guard over the inhabitants of Berwyck, then his soul would be destined to remain here for all eternity. She would not wish such a penance on Rolf and preferred to think of him resting with God's angels.

She began to cry in earnest and was so lost in her grief she was unaware when someone came from behind her and lifted her in his arms. She glanced up to see Morgan's concern for her before she buried her face into his chest. Her shoulders shook in her sorrow at the loss of her most beloved brother.

"Shhh now, lovely Coira. Rolf would not wish for you to grieve so," Morgan comforted, placing a kiss upon the top of her head. Raising her chin with his fingertips, he took his thumb and wiped at her tears falling down her cheeks.

She cried out at her loss. "I cannot help myself, Morgan. I just want to see my brother."

"My darling girl, you shall not find him buried in the ground. Look to your heart, for this is where you shall find him. Your love for him will keep his memory alive for always. You shall meet him again after you have lived a long and happy life. Such a fate is what Rolf would have wished for you."

"How can I go on without my brother, Morgan? I have no one close to me and now must needs depend on the generosity of a stranger who will make decisions about whom or when I shall marry."

"Lord Dristan is your cousin…"

"Whom I have not seen in many a year," she interjected with a frown.

"…and a fair lord, Coira," Morgan finished. "His offer to help find a husband for you is well intended. I am most grateful for any assistance he may give."

"As he did with the Lady Lynet?"

"You have heard her story?"

"Of course, I heard her story," she fumed, lifting her chin high.

"Then you know her tale has ended well," he replied, with a confident smirk.

She ignored him and tossed her hair. "I also heard about the tournament where men competed to win her hand. Is this the fate you would wish for me, Morgan?" She scowled, trying her best to convey her horror at the thought of being treated in a similar manner. And yet, would not a nunnery be an even worse fate?

Morgan had the decency to look uncomfortable. "Those were different circumstances, Coira. You are hardly in the same position as the Lady Lynet. Do not be cross with me. My heart cannot stand such a beating," he teased.

"I am not cross with you. I only feel as though I am but a pawn to be used at someone else's whim and my feelings about whom I might choose will not be considered."

"Such decisions are usually arranged for a woman. You know how these situations occur, but I give you my word I will not see you wed to some buffoon who is not worthy of you."

"Thank you, Morgan." She sniffled and rested her head upon his chest again whilst his arms once more held her close. Several minutes passed and Coira took what little comfort she found in his embrace.

Morgan whispered her name and she raised her head to stare upon him. He said not another word before leaning down to place a gentle kiss upon her lips. 'Twas not the kind of kiss that eventually would lead to future passionate encounters between them. Nay… this was but a simple kiss between two people who cared about one another as brother and sister. Nothing more… nothing less.

They broke apart, and Morgan gave her a sheepish grin. "Do not be long. I hear Lord Dristan and Lady Amiria have planned dancing for your entertainment tonight as their most honored guest."

He left her alone so she could return to her prayers. Coira was sinking back to her knees when she noticed a lone man at the edge of the forest. There was no doubt in Coira's mind the knight had just witnessed her kiss with Morgan. Such an encounter could be misconstrued, and the way the knight's fists were clenched at his side hinted that he had jumped to the wrong conclusion. So did his upset expression when he pushed off the tree he had been leaning upon, took one step in her direction, and apparently changed his mind before hurrying into the woods.

Coira followed after him, knowing she would be safe in his company. What in the world must Sir Garrick think of her after what he had just witnessed? Especially if he had felt even the smallest measure of the emotions that had consumed her since they first met.

CHAPTER 6

He was the biggest fool in all of Christendom. Garrick stormed through the woods as though hell's demons were fast on his heels. A low-lying limb from a tree slapped at his face, whacking his thick skull. He knocked the annoyance aside only for the stick to recoil and smack him once again in the back of his head. A growl of outrage ripped from his throat. He tore at the branch till it snapped in two. Cursing, he tossed it aside in his irritation to get as far away from Coira as possible.

He continued his hurried stride till he reached the edge of the forest and looked upon the beach. Mayhap, if he continued his walk along the shoreline, he would find the solace his soul was seeking. Or would he?

He would have a devil of a time whilst he attempted to erase the memory of her kissing another man, let alone how Morgan continuously held her close whenever they were together. Though brief, Garrick had shared such a pleasant encounter with the Lady Coira, he had foolishly hoped more might come of it. Garrick would admit, if only to himself, he had thought of little else since he had held Coira in his arms. She seemed to belong there, or mayhap he only imaged the feeling in the deepest recesses of his heart. No woman had ever had such an effect on him before now.

They may not have had much speech together, but if she were to be living here at Berwyck, certainly they would have plenty of time to get to know one another and perchance come to an agreement between them. He never thought she may have all ready been spoken for, but he should have known better. As Rolf's sister, she would be expected to marry within her station and not to someone like him, a mere piper for the clan. He was no knight, as she had assumed. He had only been training with the other guardsmen as Dristan commanded.

A shriek rent the air and, without thought, Garrick began to run back through the forest. A woman's scream for help continued to echo through the trees, causing him to hasten his stride. He knew not what type of danger the woman was facing but 'twas indeed dire, considering the high-pitched wail he approached by the second.

His sword drawn, Garrick was ready to meet whatever adversary he must to rescue the poor maiden. He came upon the view of slim shapely legs dangling from a tree whilst the woman attempted to secure her position in the safety of a sturdy oak. He looked around but saw nothing of concern.

"Sir Garrick! You have come to my rescue again," Coira cried out, once she sat firmly on the branch and quickly rearranged her dress to cover herself. "I am so relieved to see you."

Garrick returned his sword to the scabbard at his side. He gazed around for some unseen danger but once more saw nothing. "And just what am I rescuing ye from, my lady?" he asked. His brows crossed in confusion. Was Rolf's sister daft, perchance?

"'Twas a hideous and vile thing…"

"What was?"

"…and huge!" she continued with a terrified look. "Surely you can see that for yourself? Please slay the beast with your sword."

He leaned his palm upon the bark of the tree and looked up at her. She appeared scared, but she also never looked lovelier, at least in his eyes. "Lady Coira," he began in a calm tone. "What exactly am I protecting ye from?"

Her eyes searched the ground around the bottom of the tree before she at last pointed behind her. "'Tis just there. Can you not see that monster of a snake?"

Garrick attempted not to laugh, drew his sword and began poking around the low shrubbery. He at last saw Coira's *monster* slithering away, minding its own business. He picked up the snake with the tip of his blade before giving the reptile a toss to ease the lady's mind.

Coira gave a sigh of relief. "You should have killed the beast so 'twould not harm another venturing in the woods," she scolded.

"'Twas a harmless reptile, my lady. Besides, where else should a snake be living except in a forest? Ye are treading in their territory when ye venture tae take a walk amongst the trees. Truly, such a little animal would not have done ye harm."

"Are you sure?"

"Aye, Lady Coira."

A short snort followed by a muffled laugh had Garrick staring up at the lady perched above his head. "Well… if you are certain. I feel silly now for making such a fuss, but thank you for saving me again, Sir Knight."

"'Tis a pleasure tae be of service tae ye once more, my lady," Garrick said, again not correcting her assumption he had been knighted. He should do so whilst they had the rare opportunity of being alone. Still, he could not forget the earlier scene he had witnessed just a short time ago and mayhap 'twould do no harm to let her think on him favorably for a short while longer. "Let us see what we can do about getting ye out of the tree now, shall we?"

Coira began to scoot off the branch whilst attempting to keep her skirts in place. Garrick lifted his arms to catch her, but suddenly, Coira lost her grip on the tree. Another startled scream was torn from her lips as she began to fall.

Garrick once more captured the woman in his arms as they fell to the ground in a heap. In a repeat performance, he rolled to bear the brunt of the impact till she was captured beneath him. Hazel eyes stared at him in wonder, and his heart lurched in his chest.

"Sir Garrick…" His name passed her lips in a breathy whisper.

"Lady Coira…" he answered and, before common sense returned to him, he leaned down and placed his lips upon her own.

By God's Bones, he must be mad, he thought even as her arms pressed their way over his shoulders and wrapped themselves around his neck. His mouth moved over hers gently for he did not wish to scare her. 'Twas an exploration… a first-time meeting of two souls as their breaths exchanged with one another. He was lost, till a low throaty moan escaped her and brought him back to the reality of what he was doing.

He broke off their kiss and jumped up as though he had been burned, which was not far from the truth. *Bloody hell*! If Coira were in truth Morgan's lady, the knight would skewer him alive and see his head placed on a pike outside Berwyck's gates for taking such a liberty. He would not think about what Lord Dristan would do to his remains, since the lady was also under his watchful eye.

He began cursing and pacing back and forth, till he

realized he had left the lady of his musing lying on the hard ground. She had propped herself up on her elbows and was watching him intently. He came to her and held out his hand to help her rise. Her fingers slipped into his palm, and he once more forgot about everything else but the lady he pulled up to stand.

Her knees gave out, and she once more fell into his arms as they stumbled up against the very oak that began the downfall of his life as he knew it. Garrick reached out to steady them whilst her back pressed against the solid trunk. He clearly had no sense left in his head. He rested his arm above her head and stared down at the beautiful woman who was beginning to claim his heart.

"Coira…" he murmured. "'Tis a beautiful Gaelic name, but I am surprised an English woman is called such."

"'Twas my mother's doing. She told me years before she died that she and my father had travelled to Scotland, and she fell in love with the country and its people. She said I was a wonderful reminder of their time together."

"Ye must miss them. I am sorry for their passing, as I am for yer brother's."

"I seem to be alone in the world now," she answered softly. Garrick did not miss the small catch in her voice.

He reached out and ran the back of his finger along her cheek. "Ye are not completely alone, lass. Yer cousin will see tae yer needs," he replied, and although he hated to say the next words, he knew he must. "Ye also have Morgan. 'Tis obvious he cares for you."

"Aye, and he is the reason I followed you."

His brow rose in question. "I do not understand."

"What you saw at Rolf's gravesite is not what you think it was."

"My eyes did not deceive me. There could be no mistaking the affection he has for you." Garrick took a step back to distance himself, but she grabbed at his waist and brought him back closer to her side. "He willnae be lenient with me for being here alone with ye."

Coira reached up and ran her hand along the back of his neck. Her fingers gripped his hair. "Morgan is not my intended, Garrick," she murmured. There could be no mistaking her honest answer, nor the sincere smile she gave him.

"He is not?"

"Nay… he is merely like an older brother to me, much like Rolf. Such is the extent of our relationship. My grandfather asked Morgan to watch over me since I was not close to my cousin. I hardly know Dristan, for we did not have much contact with each other over the years whilst I was traveling with my grandfather. And Rolf and he kept their relationship a secret from the other men, for my brother did not wish it being said he was favored above others because he was Dristan's distant cousin."

Garrick frowned. "But I understood Laird Dristan's father and your own were brothers. Was I mistaken?" he asked.

"Nay, you were not. But sometimes families drift apart. After all, Lady Amiria is not close with her aunt and cousin, or so I have been told."

"But, Morgan…"

"As I said, is naught but a dear friend," she said, with a soft smile.

Relief flooded Garrick's senses as the reality of what he was experiencing with Coira exploded through him. 'Twas as though the heavens had opened to shine down upon him and anything was possible as long as this woman would be at his side.

With no further thought, he lowered his mouth towards hers.

CHAPTER 7

Coira closed her eyes and waited for the moment when Garrick would kiss her again. Her lips parted. Their breaths mingled and yet… nothing. Her eyes opened, and she gazed into green eyes as vivid as the forest around them. She could not mistake the expectation held within those flashing orbs, which mirrored her own desires.

"Are ye sure this is what ye want, sweet Coira?" he whispered, and she swooned at the way he rolled the *R* in her name with his Scottish brogue. "Just tell me tae put an end tae what we might start, and I shall let ye return tae the castle untouched."

"I cannot tell you to halt." She ran her fingers through his tawny colored hair till she urged his head forward. "I have never been more certain of anything in my entire life, Sir Knight."

'Twas all the encouragement he needed. He

swooped down and took possession of her mouth. Aye, this kiss was entirely different from the one they had shared but moments before. His mouth devoured hers with deep sweeping strokes of his tongue. Coira willingly surrendered herself to the sensations Garrick awakened in her. Since she was unsure of what would please him, she followed his lead and mimicked what he was doing, drawing his tongue further into her mouth.

He groaned deep in his throat. 'Twas a distinct primeval sound, and Coira would have smiled knowing she had pleased him, if her lips had been free to perform such a feat. He continued to plunder her mouth. 'Twas a pleasant assault on her senses she did not want to end.

The bark of the tree pushed into her back but she cared not. Her current position enabled her to revel in the awareness of every inch of her body pressed intimately against the hardness of the knight who held her tightly in his arms. Her heart furiously beat within her chest when he deepened their kiss. Surely Garrick could hear the clamor himself of what he was doing to her. She never wanted this moment to end, but how long would it be before someone came looking for her?

'Twas as though he read her thoughts as they crossed her mind, for he suddenly broke off their kiss.

Coira gasped to catch her breath, and they took their ease, foreheads gently touching. "That had to be the most perfect first kiss," she murmured, holding his shoulders for support. She knew, if she let go, she would crumble to the ground in a heap of pleasure. No one had ever made her feel so alive before.

He chuckled. "'Twas our second, if we are counting, sweet Coira."

She laughed with him and smiled, happy about what she had unexpectedly found with this man. "Aye. I suppose you have that aright, Sir Garrick."

He quickly leaned forward and placed another quick and gentle kiss upon her lips. "I am certain I am just one of many who have stolen yer kisses, Lady Coira."

Her face fell, for no one had ever looked past her ordinary face to see the inner beauty laying beneath. "Nay" she mumbled quietly. "You are the first."

He appeared surprised by her confession. "Are ye jesting with me?"

"I would not dare, kind sir." She cast her eyes downward again, embarrassed she had allowed him such a liberty but also knowing she had welcomed his touch. "I did not have anyone who pressed their suit or presented an offer of marriage. I have traveled many years with my grandfather who recently passed away. I could not leave him after all he had done for me these many years. After a while, I no longer cared if I would not marry."

"Any man would be blessed tae have ye for his wife. Ye are a dutiful lady who should be commended for her devotion tae her family."

Her eyes widened at the echo of what her grandfather said in Garrick's words. "I thank you." She swallowed hard, wondering if her grandfather would have approved of the man who had turned her world upside down with his kisses.

He traced her swollen lips with the tip of his finger, then lifted her chin to look upon her with those mesmerizing eyes she could drown in. "Ye appear as though ye have been thoroughly kissed, my lady," he murmured, with a wicked grin.

Startled, her hand flew to her mouth. "I do?"

"Aye, ye do, and I am glad tae be the one who has made ye look so."

She lost her breath with his words. Dare she hope more could possibly come to pass between them? Dare she hope these feelings within her heart could last them a lifetime? She gave a heavy sigh. "As am I, Sir Garrick," she stated, suddenly shy of being alone with him even after what they had just shared.

"We should make haste. The hour tae sup will be soon, and I know for certain ye shall be the guest of honor this eve." He offered her his elbow, and she gladly took hold of it.

"Aye, Morgan mentioned Lord Dristan and Lady Amiria had planned for minstrels to entertain us after we dine. I must admit I look forward to hearing music again." Garrick stumbled of a sudden, and Coira felt the tenseness of his arm beneath her hand. "Are you all right?" she asked with concern.

"Aye, just a misstep. We must needs hurry if we do not wish tae be late."

As they continued their way back to the castle, an awkward silence fell upon them, which seemed odd after the easiness of their earlier conversations. When they reached the steps to the keep, Garrick bowed low over her hand and excused himself without the friendliness she had become accustomed to.

"Sir Garrick," she called out. He hesitated only an instant before he turned back to await her words. "I will see you at the evening meal?" she inquired. She held her breath as she awaited his answer.

He opened and closed his mouth several times before bowing again. "Aye, my lady. I will see you then."

Her brow furrowed as she watched him depart. She entered the keep, seeking her chamber so she could change into suitable attire and spend time alone with her thoughts. As she readied herself, she wondered what in the world had changed in Garrick's demeanor. 'Twas as though he was already regretting their brief encounter in the woods.

CHAPTER 8

Garrick paced back and forth in front of the turret steps whilst he waited for Coira so they could dine together. He knew he must needs have speech with her and clear the misconception he was a knight of the realm. Their conversation earlier had startled him, leaving no doubt he should have told her the truth right then and there. Yet he could not form the words, not when he could still feel the wonderful taste of her lips.

"You do not deserve her!"

Garrick jumped as though poked with a red-hot iron when Rolf's voice whispered through his mind. "Get out of my head, Rolf," he hissed with clenched teeth.

"Stop mauling my sister and I will."

"I was not mauling her. I was kissing her," he muttered in his defense. "There is a difference."

"You have been warned."

By *God's Wounds,* now he had to worry about a ghost haunting him on top of everything else. Garrick was just about to give up his vigil at the entrance to the turret when he heard footfalls descending the stairs. He looked up in hope only to have the smile of welcome upon his face fade at what he saw.

Aye… she was beautiful, in a soft blue gown with long flowing sleeves. The white of her under tunic peeked out and was a perfect complement to the fairness of her creamy skin. Her brown hair flowed loose and tumbled down her back but 'twas her sparkling, hazel eyes when she gazed down at him that truly took his breath away.

'Twas his misfortune that said vision was being escorted down the stairs by none other than the man he had believed his rival. Although he now knew such was not the case, 'twas still bitter that he was not the one with Coira upon his arm.

Morgan was as immaculately attired as Coira. 'Twas as if the knight had known the colors the lady would wear this eve and had matched his garments to hers. If there was any doubt in Garrick's mind as to his station in life, their appearance together was a grim reminder of his place. He could in no way compete with any who had wealth aplenty and could keep this wondrous lady in the manner to which she was born. Lord Dristan would never allow him the opportunity to wed any ward he protected, let alone his cousin.

"How fine you look this eve, Sir Garrick," Coira stated, reaching out her hand when they reached the last step.

He bowed low over her fingertips. "Ye are too gracious with yer compliments, my lady."

Morgan bumped into Garrick's shoulder none too gently and made an attempt to continue through to the great hall. "Come, Coira. There is no time for idle conversations, not when the evening meal is awaiting our arrival."

She gave a merry laugh. "We are hardly late, Morgan. If you but care to look, our liege lord and his lady are not yet even in attendance."

Morgan mumbled something beneath his breath. "All the more reason to be in our places upon their arrival."

"But–"

"Garrick understands, do you not? Everyone knows their place in life and their duty." There could be no mistaking the message in the glare Morgan tossed Garrick, nor his implication.

"My lady," Garrick replied with a short bow as the couple left him standing there and made their way to the raised dais. He stood there in a stupor watching them go. He had had no opportunity to correct Coria's misconception about his status. Now she was sitting in a place of honor and he at one of the lower tables, and he had no idea how he would get a moment in private with her. 'Twas a disaster in the making.

Garrick was so lost in thought, he blindly began making his way to his seat and ran right into a small child, knocking the lad to the floor in an undignified heap. The boy lost his grip on his little wooden sword that went skittering across the stones. There was no mistaking this young pup, who was aged but seven summers and who still hid his sore backside with a glare that would one day rival his sire's.

"Ach, Royce. My apologies, laddie," Garrick said, helping the boy to rise.

"'Twas my own fault, Garrick. I should not have been running in my father's hall. You will not tell him, will you?" Royce pleaded and began looking for his sword. Finding his missing blade, he ran over and placed it into the makeshift scabbard that had been made for him, then came back to look expectedly upon Garrick.

"Nay, Royce. Yer secret is safe with me, but what were ye running from, if I may ask?" Garrick offered a wink of conspiracy to the lad.

Royce looked about the hall then motioned for Garrick to lean down to his level. "A couple of boys thought to teach me a lesson. They claim I am merely a spoiled brat and had planned to throw me in a horse trough."

Garrick gazed about the hall and saw two lads slightly older than Royce make a hasty retreat towards the kitchens. "Ye appear tae be safe for now, lad, but if the situation continues, ye must needs be sure tae talk tae yer father."

Royce's eyes widened. "He will think me weak," he declared, standing a little taller for all his youth.

Garrick knelt down to the boy's level. He could certainly understand the lad's sentiment regarding his father, but Garrick also knew the deep and abiding love Lord Dristan and Lady Amiria had for their children. "There is no shame in letting yer sire know ye are being bullied. Better tae tell him so he can set the matter straight than for harm tae come tae ye, Royce. Do I have yer word?"

"Aye, you have it, Garrick."

"Good! Now be off with ye and go chase after yer dragons and slay them to protect yer sister."

Royce laughed but pulled out his sword and made a jabbing motion at the air. "Ha! Liliana is only two summers, Garrick, and is not yet in need of protecting. Besides, I would rather you teach me how to play your bagpipes or the lute."

Garrick stood up and ruffled the boy's hair. "Maybe when yer older lad. Now go find yer place so ye can fill yer belly."

He watched the boy run off and once again was about to find his place when he felt a hand take hold of his arm. Garrick gazed down into the violet eyes of Lady Amiria.

"You are good with him," she said whilst she

watched her son make his way through the hall. "You will make a good father yourself someday."

Garrick's eyes wandered to the lady making her way through the hall. If only a marriage with Coira was possible. "Mayhap," he mumbled.

"Is Royce having trouble with those boys again?"

"Ye knew?"

She gave his arm a squeeze. "Of course we knew, but so far 'tis only the actions of boys who are jealous of their laird's son. Since Royce has always been fond of you, perchance you would be so kind as to keep an extra eye on him when you see him about?"

"Ye honor me, my lady," Garrick said with a slight bow.

"I wish you would call me by my given name, Garrick. We have been through so much during the years since our childhood together. We are, after all, part of the same clan, no matter I married an Englishman."

"All the more reason for me tae remember ye are now the lady of this hall. I care not to have yer dragon breathing his fire down my neck tae remind me of my place and the respect ye deserve."

Amiria laughed. "Yes... well... I suppose I can see your point. He does have a bit of a temper."

"Do ye think so?" he teased with a raised brow.

She watched him with those knowing violet eyes of hers for several moments till she gazed about her hall. They began to walk. "You need to tell her, Garrick, and quickly. You know you are expected to play for us this eve."

Garrick stopped in his stride to gaze down upon the lady he had known since his youth. There was not much he could hide from her. "Ye also know I care for her?" His eyes traveled to the raised dais where Morgan was helping Coira sit. No matter where she was, Garrick could always easily find the lady his heart yearned to make his own.

She smiled again before reaching up to pat his cheek. "I am happy love has found you, my friend, but such love is on shaky ground when you begin with a misunderstanding. You will need to plead your case to Dristan in any event, but your first obstacle will be to right Coira's perception of you."

"'Twas not done intentionally, and then there seemed no opportunity tae fix the problem."

"You have run out of time, Garrick. You best right the matter as soon as the meal is finished or the whole hall will witness her disappointment."

"I can already hear the heckling of *the lady and the piper*. Even Rolf does not approve."

"Rolf has no say where his sister's heart may lead her. I see nothing wrong with you caring for the lady, and from the looks I have seen her give you, I know she cares for you, too."

"Ye think I may have a chance tae win the lady's heart."

"Aye, just as long as she hears from you that you are

our clan's piper. Do not let her feel embarrassed by her mistake and assumption by learning the truth from others, Garrick."

Garrick nodded and left Amiria's side to head toward the kitchen to confront the two boys and perchance give them a fair warning to leave their laird's son alone. He was about to enter when the whisperings of the servants met his ears.

"She be a true lady, that one is. No uppity airs, no demanding ways. She does her deceased brother proud, she does," boasted one of the servants.

"Bah!" Fira fumed and Garrick watched in surprise when she slammed a pitcher down upon the table. Garrick had avoided the woman, knowing she had developed an attraction to him. He never felt the same about her, and he knew she had already been with several of Laird Dristan's knights. What was she so upset about?

Another woman replied, with a shudder, "Do not forget she is Laird Dristan's cousin and as such 'twould be wise tae treat her with respect lest ye wish tae feel the heat o' the Devil's Dragon's wrath."

Fira wagged her finger at the women, who had no issue gossiping amongst themselves. "She dinnae belong here and should go back tae France or wherever Sir Morgan found her."

"Yer just jealous because ye have lost the favor o' our handsome piper."

"I havenae lost him," Fira boasted, "and I can have him in my bed with a crook of my finger, I can."

The kitchen servants burst into laughter, causing Garrick to frown. He did not appreciate being a part of their gossip.

"Ye may get him in yer bed, but yer reward will likely be a babe in yer belly and nothing else," a woman called out.

"He willnae marry ye, ye silly girl." Another chorus of laughter erupted from those near enough to hear the conversation.

One of the other women said, "I have heard Laird Dristan will look no lower than a knight fer her husband."

Fira's smirk could be heard in her reply. "Then 'tis settled. Since Garrick holds no title, he is considered beneath her station in life, so our laird willnae let them marry."

"Ye think that matters when yer in love? Ye best set yer sights on someone else fer 'tis plain fer all tae see Lady Coira has won Garrick's heart."

"Ye know nothing of Garrick's heart," Fira yelled.

"Then take a look the next time they are together," the woman mocked. "Only someone who is blind wouldnae notice they have fallen fer one another.

"Yer wrong," Fira all but shouted.

"Heed my words, Fira, and leave him be. Another has already claimed him," the woman taunted afore returning to her work.

Garrick left before he was discovered, confronting the boys now all but forgotten. He took his place at the table with some of Amiria's guardsmen. A goblet was thrust into his hand but he barely tasted the heady brew. His eyes focused on the lovely woman at the raised dais. When the lady raised her chalice in a silent salute, Garrick returned the gesture with a smile. His happiness was short lived when Fira brushed by him with tear-filled eyes.

Guilt wracked his body for unknowingly hurting Fira but more so that he had left Coira ignorant of who he was. He must speak with her posthaste. Food barely passed his lips, for he had no stomach to eat when he knew what must needs be done and quickly. He simply needed to figure out a way to get her from Morgan's side so he might have a private word with her. Such an obstacle might be the end of him.

CHAPTER 9

Coira observed Morgan as he finished off what was left of the food on the trencher they had been sharing. There was still an overabundance of victuals before her that had barely been touched. She had picked at her own portion of the meal but found she had no appetite. Her mind continued to wander to one knight in particular sitting amongst the warriors who protected Berwyck's walls. She felt his stare and when their eyes met across the crowded hall, her heart leapt within her chest. She smiled in his direction, and he gave her a slight nod.

"He is not good enough for you," Morgan muttered, reaching over to fill her side of the trencher, "and you should eat lest you fall over in a faint. A bird eats more than you have this eve."

Coira took a small nibble to appease the man next

to her. "Will there be any man worthy of me in your eyes, Morgan?" she asked him with a raised brow.

"Nay."

"Sir Garrick is a fine man," she retaliated.

"Bah! You do not even know him," he snapped, his brow furrowing in suppressed annoyance.

"I know him well enough that I can honestly say I care for him." Coira pushed the food with her utensil around on the trencher. Could she really feel something for Sir Garrick in such a short amount of time?

"Nay, you do not, for he has not told you…" he clamped his lips shut.

Lady Amiria leaned forward to interrupt. "Morgan, 'tis not your place."

Morgan reached for his chalice and took a sip. "She needs to know, my lady."

"And she shall hear it for herself from Garrick."

"'Twould be far better for her to have a nobleman to marry to keep her in the manner to which she is accustomed and not—"

"Leave it be, Morgan," Amiria warned with a scowl.

Coira looked between the pair, who now remained tight-lipped. She could not stand their silence. "What is this secret you two are keeping from me?" They did not reply, which only irritated Coira for she could not figure out what was going on around her.

Any further attempts to partake of the evening meal were gone, for Coira could not do anything more than drink her wine. Soon, the food was cleared, and the tables began to be moved in order to allow for dancing. Garrick began to make his way towards the raised dais, and she hoped he would ask for the first dance.

"Play us a tune, Piper," someone in the hall called out, causing Garrick to flinch before sliding to a halt in the middle of the room. He gazed in her direction, his face stricken with grief, but why?

"Aye, mayhap the lute this eve," another nameless face beckoned. "At least we know you play better than you fight with a sword."

The hall erupted in laughter but Coira did not join in their merriment. 'Twas at last clear to Coira. She had made a horrible mistake by assuming Garrick had earned his spurs. He was the clan piper and not a knight of honor! She had been made a fool, and everyone within the hall knew of her foolish misunderstanding.

A sob tore past her lips and, before Morgan or Lady Amiria could stop her, she fled the room. She ignored her name being called out as she ascended up the turret stairs on slippered feet. If only she could reach the sanctity of her room, but 'twas not to be for Garrick easily caught up with her. She began to run down the passageway.

"Coira! Wait," he bellowed.

"Leave me alone," she roared, continuing her way towards her chambers. She reached for the latch and entered the portal. As she went to slam the door shut, he forced his way inside and slid the bolt.

"Get out of my chamber!"

"Nay," Garrick pleaded holding out his hands, "not till ye let me right the wrong I have done."

She pointed towards the door. "You made me the laughing stock of the entire castle, Garrick. How could you let me go on believing you were a knight?"

"I am most sorry, Lady Coira, but I meant tae tell ye. I just couldnae find the right time."

"Surely you jest, sir! You do not think you could have told me earlier this day when we were alone in the forest?"

"I had my mind on other things," he muttered but had the decency to appear ashamed.

A sarcastic laugh erupted from Coira. "Oh… aye… I know exactly what you were thinking."

"I willnae regret kissing ye in the forest, Coira," he answered. A worried frown marred his handsome face. "I know 'twas wrong of me tae not put an end tae yer assumption I was a knight."

"You should have been the one to tell me," she snarled, poking her finger into his chest. He caught her hand and pulled her into his arms. "Let go of me."

"We shall have this out now between us."

"Nay, we will not," she said trying to push at his chest. 'Twas like attempting to move a wall of stone. He budged not even an inch. "You all have been jesting with me, making me appear the fool. How shall I ever show my face outside this room again?"

"No one thinks such of ye, my sweet Coira," Garrick replied, brushing her cheek.

Her eyes widened, even whilst her traitorous heart beat faster at hearing the endearment. She would not give him the satisfaction of forgiving him. "I am not *your* Coira."

He backed her up against the door. "Aye... ye are."

She watched in fascination and horror as his head began to lower, and he closed his eyes. "Do not dare ki—"

Her words were cut off as his mouth descended upon hers. She did everything in her power to not respond and was watching when Garrick's eyes flew open. He stepped back as if he realized his error... again.

She advanced upon him. "Do not think you can easily kiss away the hurt you have inflicted upon me this day. Please leave my chamber, Garrick."

"Ye cannae deny there be something between us, lass." He tried again to approach her, but she held up her hand.

"Get out," she snapped out sharply.

Garrick made his way to the door and slid the bolt. Flinging open the door, he came face to face with Lord Dristan and Morgan, their expressions grim.

"Are you all right, Lady Coira?" Lord Dristan asked gruffly.

"Aye," Coira stated choking back a sob. "Garrick was just leaving."

Garrick looked back over his shoulder towards her. "We will have speech on the morrow, Coira, so I may set the matter aright between us."

Lord Dristan took hold of Garrick's tunic and pulled him into the passageway. "I believe you must needs have a conversation with your liege lord before you have any discussion with the Lady Coira. Get thee to my solar, Garrick."

Coira watched them depart, leaving Morgan standing in the portal with clenched fists. "Did he harm you?"

Coira walked to the door with steadier feet than she thought she was capable of. "Not in the way you may think, Morgan." At his quizzical look, she shook her head. "I will be fine. I just want my privacy. I am sure you understand."

She did not give him any further explanations but shut the door and slid the bolt. Far into the evening she sat upon the edge of her bed, wondering how she could have made such a foolish mistake. How would she ever be able to save face in the eyes of those who lived within Berwyck's walls?

She continued her vigil until dawn lit the furthest reaches of the eastern sky. One thing weighed more heavily on her mind than her embarrassment and her pain. Try as she might, she could see no way to resolve the obstacle now before her. For how would Lord Dristan ever consent for her, a lady of the realm, to marry a mere clan piper? 'Twas an impossible situation, and one that sealed her fate of never being able to marry for love.

CHAPTER 10

Garrick continued his vigilant morning prayers even whilst the chapel emptied of those seeking Father Donovan's blessings and absolutions of their sins. Head bowed, his fingers clutched at the book of prayers given to him by his grandmother on the day he had turned ten and eight. He brought the book upwards and tapped the cover against his forehead. She would be disappointed in him if she yet lived.

He had known he had been in the wrong to not tell Coira the truth about his status within the clan. He had been so taken by her and so afraid she would no longer see him in the same light once she found out the truth. May God above forgive him. He was unsure he would ever be able to erase the hurt in her eyes. 'Twould haunt him to the end of his days.

His conversation several nights ago with his liege

lord also weighed heavily on his mind. Laird Dristan had made it perfectly clear Garrick was to keep his distance from his ward. The berating he had received had reminded Garrick of his place within the clan and Laird Dristan's household, despite the extra training he had been receiving without anyone's knowledge. Never, in all his life till now, had Garrick wished he was a true knight of the realm. His wishes had changed, but his status had not. His deepest desire, to be Lady Coira's husband, appeared unattainable.

Garrick once more turned to his prayers, but no matter how hard he asked for forgiveness, he knew within him only one person would be able to ease the pain within his soul. Unfortunately, Coira would have nothing to do with him. Days had passed, and yet he had been told she refused to leave her chambers. How could he profess his love for her if she refused to see him? He was doomed.

"You really do care for her." Rolf's voice whispered through his mind, and Garrick's head rose from his prayers.

"Aye, Sir Rolf, I do indeed." Garrick looked about the chapel and watched in amazement when a smoky distortion began to take shape in the form of a lone knight long since gone from the land of the living.

"You will cost me much for appearing to you as I am," Rolf declared, looking as real as if he in truth sat next to him on the bench.

Garrick reached out his hand, but his fingers went

straight through the apparition at his side. 'Twas then he realized he had heard Rolf's voice out loud. "Am I dead?" he asked in alarm. He quickly made the sign of the cross.

Rolf chuckled. "Nay, but you will be if you harm one hair upon my sister's head."

"I have no desire tae have ye haunting me fer the rest of my days, Sir Rolf. Yer sister's happiness is all I desire."

"You seem sincere enough, and 'tis all I ask of you."

"Are ye, mayhap, giving me yer blessing?"

Rolf sighed. "From what I have witnessed, your souls are bound to one another. Perchance you have met in another place in time. I, for one, will not stand in your way, as long as you make things right with Coira."

"She willnae have speech with me," Garrick grumbled.

"Do you blame her?"

"Nay, but her distance makes it nigh impossible for me tae apologize."

Rolf observed him for several minutes before he apparently came to some decision. "She is currently walking up on the battlement walls. I will see what I can do on your behalf. Perchance by the time you make your way there yourself, she will hear you plead your case."

"Ye would perform such a service for me?" Garrick asked, as Rolf's form faded in the light of the chapel.

"I would do anything for the man my sister loves."

As Rolf's words registered in Garrick's mind, he gave another word of prayer and thanks, feeling hopeful for the first time in days that mayhap all would work out as it should.

~

COIRA CAREFULLY strode along the narrow parapet walkway, lost in thought. 'Twas the first day she at last felt 'twas time she left her chamber and sought the fresh air to calm her frayed nerves. She was as much to blame for her folly as Garrick. She had come to such a revelation only this morn. Why it had taken so long for her to admit her own mistake was beyond her ken.

She had purposefully stayed away from Garrick. She feared once she laid eyes upon him, she would make a spectacle of herself by throwing herself into his arms, begging for forgiveness. How was she to approach him now? How was it possible to go back and start anew?

Coria leaned her forearms on the stone wall to peer down below into the inner bailey. Beyond the curtain wall, she could see the stretch of beach with the ocean waves crashing into the shore. A feeling of peace overwhelmed her till she shivered as though something had whispered across her soul.

She blinked as the very air before her distorted. Try as she might, she could in no way calm her breathing.

What in heaven's name was she witnessing? Was she perchance losing her mind? The vision continued to take shape. She gave a startled gasp of surprise and fell to her knees in disbelief when she saw her beloved brother appear.

"Rolf! Do my eyes deceive me? How is this possible you are standing before me?" she asked, a sob of joy escaped her.

He gave her a sad sort of smile before he raised his eyes heavenward. "My Lord God, please grant my humble request to hold my sister just this once," he murmured in a fervent prayer. As though in answer, a beam of light came from the skies above and shone down upon Coira.

Rolf held out his hand, and Coira grabbed ahold of his fingers before she was hauled into the waiting arms of her brother. "Oh Rolf! 'Tis a miracle," she cried out giving him a fierce hug.

"Aye but one that will not last but an instant. Let me look at you." He cupped her face and placed a kiss upon each cheek. "Just as lovely, if not more so, than I remember."

She laughed. "You are jesting with me, my dearest Rolf. You know you were always the good looking one in the family. My face is rather plain and not one the bards would praise in song," she teased.

"You are beautiful to me and always have been," he murmured. "How I have missed you, my sweet sister."

Coira was hauled back into his arms, and yet she

could feel his grip lessening around her. She clasped him tighter till she stumbled when his form once more turned into but a vague whisper of an image. She tried to cover her disappointment with a timid smile. "I suppose to have you hold me even for just a moment is better than to never have done so at all," she said, tears brimming in her eyes at such a gift. Her feelings were a jumbled mess. Her great relief when her brother appeared to her warred with her sadness as he became a ghost once more.

"I will have a hard time recovering from all I have done this day in order to have those whom I care about see me in such a state," he answered, with the cocky smile she was used to seeing in Rolf's visage.

"Then you must have a message of grave import if you are appearing before me, although I had hoped you would at some time whilst I remained here at Berwyck. The servants fear you."

"Bah! I have given them no cause to do so."

"'Tis said you haunt the place and will not move on."

"'Twas a small price to pay so I might look after those I left behind."

"Like me?" Her voice shook, and she wished she could once again have her brother hold her in his arms, but 'twas not to be.

"Aye," he confessed, but Coira could see him beginning to fade and knew he would not be with her for much longer, "but only for as long as you remain at Berwyck, for I am bound to the castle grounds."

"I am not certain I can stay here, although I have no idea where else I might go."

"Berwyck is a fine place to call home, Coira, and Dristan is family. You may not have had much of an opportunity to know him in your youth, but he will care for you on my behalf."

"His reputation has preceded him. I am somewhat afraid of him, as are those who serve him," she stated with a shudder.

"Dristan's reputation is mostly from those who have met him upon the battlefield. Most of what you hear is no more than rumor. He is hardly the fierce, fire-breathing dragon you might imagine him to be," Rolfe teased, then continued. "But do not let him know I have told you this. Our liege lord does not want his people to believe he is getting soft."

She gave a light laugh. "If you say so, then it must be true."

Rolf gave her a smile. "You shall be happy here, Coira, but only because of a certain man who cares for you."

Coira watched her brother perch himself on the ledge of the parapet wall, not that he had a need to do so, given his current state of being. "You are speaking of Garrick, I suppose."

"I certainly did not mean Morgan, although he, too, cares for your well-being." Rolf folded his arms across his chest.

Coira rubbed at her eyes. "Garrick and I have fallen into disaccord," she mumbled.

"Then make amends. 'Twill not be hard for you both to do so."

Her brow rose at his implication. "You think 'twill be so easy to forgive him?"

"He must needs forgive you as well, Coira. 'Tis not his fault you assumed he was one of Dristan's knights. Forgiving each other will be a good beginning for you both. Besides, I have given him my blessing and he will be here shortly, so you will need to decide your fate quickly."

She put her hands upon her hips and made an attempt to appear stern, causing her brother to laugh as he did in their youth. "'Tis nice of you to decide on my behalf who I will wed, brother. I am not sure we can fix the problem facing us so easily. Not without Dristan's blessing."

"Only a blind man could not see for himself how you are both connected. He will make you happy, Coira, if you but give him the chance to prove his love to you," Rolf declared.

Coira gave a heavy sigh. "I suppose you see things us mere mortals here upon earth cannot, so I must needs take your word for it."

Rolf said not a word. He rose, and drew close to hover in the air at her side. He reached out to touch her cheek, and Coira felt her face tingling. "I will always be near, sweet sister. Keep me forever in your heart."

Before Coira could answer him, he was gone, fading into a hint of smoky vapor. Her knees buckled with his disappearance, whilst tears rushed down her cheeks. She had just had an encounter with her deceased brother! She had no further time to ponder her brother's miraculous appearance before she heard the turret door open. Turning, she saw Garrick's approach and knew he already owned her heart.

CHAPTER 11

Garrick had almost reached the turret door when he encountered Fira on the narrow stairs. Their eyes briefly met when they passed one another but he had no time to worry over the troublesome look she gave him. He had bigger problems on his mind than to wonder what she was doing so far from Berwyck's kitchen.

Coira was standing on the parapet and Garrick observed Coira's reaction when he appeared through the turret portal. Any hint of remaining anger was quickly replaced with relief he had sought her out… or at least, 'twas Garrick's wish she was happy to see him.

Garrick went to her. Taking her hands, he began to rub the coolness from her fingers. "Can ye forgive me, Coira, for not telling ye the truth myself?"

Coira gave a heavy sigh. "I am as much to blame as you are, Garrick."

He continued to rub his thumb across her hand. "Then we must needs forgive one another and go forward. 'Tis the only way for us tae begin anew."

A tear slid slowly down her cheek and hc took a moment to wipe it away with a kiss.

"'Tis hopeless, Garrick," she sobbed.

"Doonae worry yerself, lass. We shall think of something," he whispered, and suddenly found his arms full when his lady reached out to him for support. He could do nothing less but clutch her trembling body to his own. "Please, Coira… I cannae stand yer tears."

"If my cousin will not give his consent for us to wed, he will marry me to another. How will I bear it?"

How indeed, he thought remembering once again his meeting with Laird Dristan. His laird had warned Garrick that his life would be all but over if he so much as touched the hem of Coira's gown. And now here he was with his arms wrapped around his lady offering her what comfort he could.

"Hush now, my sweet. Dry yer eyes. I willnae have this upsetting ye." Coira lifted her head and he looked into her tear-filled eyes. He swore his heart broke all over again and he could not imagine a life without this woman at his side. He pushed back a lock of her hair that fell across her face and laid a kiss upon her forehead.

"I cannot marry another, Garrick," she said, echoing his own thoughts, "not when my heart's desire is to belong only to you."

"'Twill not come to that, I promise ye."

"You cannot make such a vow, Garrick, and I will not hold you to it. You know my cousin better than most. When his mind is made up, he will not change it. He had decided I will marry no less than a knight. How are we to move on, Garrick?" She groaned, pulling her hands from his and placing them behind her back.

"We shall think of something," he answered, despite his doubt they would be able to find a solution to their problem. When all was said and done, he still held no title and had no right to wed a noblewoman.

"I am still the ward of Lord Dristan. Do you honestly think he will readily give my hand in marriage?" Her words echoed his thoughts.

"Ye mean to a lowly clan piper?" he fumed, turning from her, afraid in his anger he might say something he would regret. Still, his words rushed out of his mouth before he could stop them. "'Tis obvious ye do not wish tae be called the piper's lady but feel ye must needs hold out for a higher, lofty title."

"If you knew me at all, then you would know a title has little meaning to me. Such a status never did. I measure a person not by their status in life but by how they treat others, myself included," she snapped lifting her chin in defiance.

He conceded her point with a short nod, for they had not really spent much time together having speech about their lives and how they had lived. "Again, I apologize for my words. I can plead my cause tae Laird

Dristan. He and his lady will understand we have feelings for one another."

Her brow rose at his words. "And do you have feelings for me, Garrick?"

"How can ye doubt me… or us, for that matter?"

"'Tis a near impossible situation we find ourselves in. I cannot change who I am and that I am expected to marry a nobleman," Coira retorted sadly.

"Is this what you want? Tae marry someone else?" Garrick asked, his heart faltering at the thought of Coira belonging to another man.

She covered her face with her hands. "The thought of marrying any man, no less a complete stranger, never even occurred to me. I never expected to marry at all, for who would want me for his wife?" she bawled.

"I would. I will make him see reason, Coira, and prove my worth upon the lists," Garrick proclaimed. "Trust me…"

She gave a heavy sigh. "You know I do with my very life, Garrick. Now kiss me as a token of your affection, for I must needs return to Amiria's solar before I am missed." She closed her eyes and leaned back her head.

He wasted no time claiming the lady's lips, and she more than proved her own desires when he deepened their kiss. He was unsure how long they stood there wrapped up in their own little world, but the sound of Coira's name being called from the turret stairs broke the spell woven around them. Not wishing to be caught openly disobeying his liege lord, he reluctantly set Coira back from his arms.

"I must go," she declared, even though her eyes told him she would rather stay. "I will see you at the evening meal."

He could only nod in response, not trusting himself to have further speech with the lady. Instead, he watched her leave to disappear down the stairway. Garrick leaned his arms against the battlement wall, lost in thought, till he felt a hand upon his arm. He did not expect to see Fira at his side. Her eyes were swimming pools of jealousy, for she clearly could not mask the emotions etched upon her mutinous face.

"What is it, Fira?" he asked, almost hating to hear her answer. She had been bothersome of late with hopes that there was something between them. He was unsure where she had gotten such a notion for he had been nothing but polite to her in the past.

"What does that outsider have that I do not?" Fira hissed, reaching for his arm. He pried her fingers away but she only stepped closer.

"I willnae discuss the Lady Coira with ye," he answered, hoping she would let the matter rest. Such was not going to be the case.

"Ye shall regret not taking me up on my offer, Garrick. 'Tis best tae stay with yer own kind instead of thinking ye can wed someone above yer station."

Garrick scowled, her words thrusting into his heart like a dagger. He did not need Fira to remind him that he was only the clan's piper and not a knight. "Doonae be daft, Fira. I have already told ye I am not interested in what ye offer tae any of the men who pass through Berwyck's gates. Be off with ye and mind yer own business." His voice was harsh as he lost what little patience he had left.

Fira gave a bitter laugh. "Ye best remember my words, Garrick," she answered leaning her shoulder upon the wall and crossing her arms.

"If ye willnae leave me in peace, then stay and enjoy yer view," Garrick huffed. He gave her no further thought and made his way back to the lists. He would pour every ounce of energy he possessed into proving to Laird Dristan he was worthy to wed the fair Coira.

CHAPTER 12

Coira had begun to lose hope of ever having a relationship with Garrick. There had been no more time for stolen moments together, not when Dristan kept her under close watch. Several knights had begun showing up at Berwyck's gates at Dristan's invitation. They were here to court her and, on the surface, went out of their way to win her favor. But no matter how gallant they appeared to be, Coira learned for herself they were only interested in being connected to King Henry's champion knight. They praised her cousin any chance they could, and discussed her dowry when they thought she wasn't listening. 'Twas clear they were only interested in the connections and wealth they would attain by wedding Coira.

Dristan grumbled when Coira turned one man down after the other. With Amiria's help at soothing her fiery dragon's temper, he began to back down on his efforts to find Coira a husband, at least for now. He said he would widen his search to find her a proper husband. She would enjoy this short reprieve whilst she had it, knowing her cousin's relentless quest to see Coira properly wed.

She leaned back against the wall behind the stone bench on which she sat to watch the men training in the lists. A sense of *déjà vu* brought a smile to her face. She remembered the first time she had seen Garrick upon the training field. He was just as magnificent now as he had been months ago, mayhap even more so. He had poured every spare moment into his training in his attempt to prove to her cousin he would be worthy of her, and his efforts were paying off.

Her eyes lovingly moved down the entire length of his body and she suppressed a moan at what she saw. Garrick was shirtless, allowing her gaze to all but devour every inch of his lean muscled stomach. Sweat glistened upon his skin whilst he continued to swing his sword in long even strokes. Watching him now, she would have never guessed he was the clan's piper. He appeared every inch a trained knight of Berwyck's garrison guards.

Another low moan threatened to escape her lips as desire for the man she cared for made her body tingle in response. If they did not wed soon, she swore she might make a fool of herself and beg the man to bed her. 'Twas a sin, she knew, but she cared less and less about her virginity. She only wished to claim Garrick as her husband. But how were they to convince her cousin they should wed? She did not care if she became known as the piper's lady.

"Ye should go back tae where ye came from," hissed a woman who had crept up on Coira whilst her attention had been riveted on Garrick's magnificent form. The woman's eyes radiated enough animosity that Coria instantly knew this woman hated her but why? Coira recognized the young woman as one of the castle servants.

Confused, Coira peered closely at the woman, as though she should know what the girl was blabbering about. "Excuse me?"

"Go home! Ye dinnae belong here," she fumed, with fists clenched at her side.

Coira came to a stand as she began to understand that perchance the woman also held an affection for a certain clan piper.

"You are Fira, are you not?" she inquired softly, hoping to put the girl at ease. She did not wish to have any enemies within the castle. The woman served her food and 'twas anyone's guess what this girl might plan for her. However, Coira would also not let anyone intimidate her and belittle what she felt for Garrick.

"Aye," Fira answered, taking deep gulping breaths of air as if to calm her growing anger.

"Berwyck is my home, Fira. Did you not hear Lord

Dristan's announcement that he is my cousin?" Coira asked.

"Ye cannae have him," she shouted when her emotions got the best of her.

"Are you speaking of Garrick?"

"Of course, I am speaking of Garrick. He is mine." Fira made the proclamation with a toss of her head.

So... Coira was right in her assumption that Fira was in love with the man too. "Garrick is honorable, is he not?" she inquired with a small smile.

"Aye! He is one of the most honorable men I have ever met." Fira's smirk boasted a confidence that would be fleeting.

"Then you must agree with me that Garrick would never carelessly give his attention to another if he truly cared for someone."

Fira's mouth opened and closed several times as though she was attempting to find a fitting response. "Ye cannae have him," she repeated, although this time her words were barely above a whisper. Tears began to leak from her eyes.

"I believe that is for Garrick alone to decide," Coira responded. Before Fira could reply, Amiria came running toward the lists.

"Dristan! Garrick!" she called out as she came to stand next to Coira. "Fira! What are you doing so far from the kitchen? Get back to work." Fira left, with tears streaming down her face.

Dristan and Garrick quickly came to their side.

"What is the matter, wife?" Dristan asked, glaring at Garrick for standing entirely too close to Coira.

"'Tis Royce. I cannot find him anywhere," Amiria said before being crushed into her husband's embrace. "I have been searching nigh unto an hour. No one has seen him since the noon meal."

Coira stood silent whilst watching the couple before her. Both so strong yet concern for their child left them both helpless. A small price to pay for the responsibility of parenthood.

Garrick put on his tunic and took Coira's hand. She held on tightly, not caring if Dristan saw this display of affection. "We shall find him, my lady," Garrick replied. "He cannae have gone far."

Dristan called out to his knights. "My son has gone missing. Scour the surrounding area of the castle, the forest, even the beach. I want him found before the evening meal!"

Knights scattered as if their fire-breathing dragon had scorched the ground behind them, and their tails with it. Coira watched them leave before turning her gaze to Garrick.

"I want to help find Royce," she whispered to the man who still clasped her hand in his. He placed a kiss upon her knuckles.

"By yer leave, my laird," Garrick said, standing tall and proud as though to give Dristan the opportunity to berate him for touching his ward.

"Granted. You know the lad better than most." He

pointed his finger sternly between the two of them. "But do not think we shall not be discussing whatever this is going on between you and Lady Coira."

"I love him, Dristan," Coira said, with a confidence that proved her words were true.

"Bah! You barely know one another," Dristan insisted with a scowl.

"I love him," she reaffirmed, lifting her chin.

Dristan's brow rose. "As I said… we shall discuss this later… *after* my son has been found."

Coira smiled and loosened her grip on Garrick's hand to stand before her cousin. Amiria smiled at her and gave her a wink, even though Coira could see how concerned she was for her son.

Coira rose up on her toes and placed a kiss on Dristan's cheek. "I love you too, cousin."

Dristan grumbled some sort of a reply but Coira was already grasping Garrick's hand as they hastened in the search for Royce. Where could the boy have gone?

CHAPTER 13

Knowing the outside perimeter of the castle was being carefully search by the garrison knights, Garrick pulled Coira with him to search the keep once more. The lad could be hiding anywhere but, somewhere in the back of his mind, Garrick had the feeling Royce was in trouble.

They were half way across the great hall when they encountered Kenna, Berwyck's healer. She rushed toward them and grasped Garrick's arm. The woman swayed, eyes rolling back in her head before she began to fall.

"Kenna," Coira called out reaching for the woman.

"Dinnae touch her, Coira," Garrick warned. "She has the sight and touching her may cause her to spin in an entirely different direction."

"As you wish, Garrick," she replied, as she lowered herself next to Kenna on the floor.

Garrick looked up to espy Fira near the kitchen. "Fira! Find Sir Geoffrey and tell him his wife will need him."

"Ye cannae order me about!" she said with pursed lips.

"Not now, Fira. Please do as I ask," Garrick ordered and watched her leave to deliver his message… or so he hoped.

Garrick and Coira continued to carefully watch over Kenna, unable to do anything till her vision had passed. 'Twas not the first time that Garrick had witnessed such an occurrence, although Kenna rarely had anything of import to pass onto him.

Several minutes passed till Kenna's eyes began to flutter open. "Garrick… 'tis Royce!

"Do ye ken where he is, Kenna?" he asked, worry etching his brow.

"'Tis dark and cold," she began. "He cannae move for someone has tied him up. The poor lad is scared, Garrick. Ye must find him!"

"Let us get ye near a chair by the hearth. Can ye stand, Kenna?" he inquired.

"Aye… with a wee bit of help," she said.

With Garrick on one side and Coira on the other, they helped her to her feet, and they made their way through the remainder of the hall.

"Go find him, Garrick," Kenna replied, with a wave of her hand once she was seated. "I know ye have sent for my husband. I shall be fine till he arrives."

"Are you sure, Kenna?" Coira asked.

"Aye! Off with the two of ye. I can fend for myself, which is more than can be said for the boy."

Garrick knew where to search first. As they made their way toward the rear of the kitchen, he halted before a door that led far below into the depths of the keep. He turned toward Coira. "'Tis a foul place I am going. Mayhap ye should stay here."

Coira protested. "Nay! I go where you go, Garrick. Lead the way."

He took her hand and descended the narrow stairs leading farther and farther below to the dungeons of the keep. He grabbed a torch from one of the sconces on the wall and began peering into the empty cells.

"Royce!" he called out, and the boy's name echoed eerily in the underground rooms. There was no answer and Garrick swore. He had been certain this is where the boy would have been hidden.

"What is that? Coira said, pointing to a place on the floor with metal bars over the hole so no one would accidently fall into it.

"God forbid if they threw the lad into that hideous pit!" Garrick fumed. He called out for the boy and waved the torch over the hole. But there was only minor scurrying of whatever rodents occupied the pit and no sign of Royce.

A sigh of relief left Coira's lips. "Thank goodness he is not down there."

"Aye, I am glad of it as well. But where else tae

look?" He took Coira's hand and returned the torch to the sconce. They began making their way back up the stairs.

"Think, Garrick. You must know where someone might have taken him."

"There is only one other place, but I dinnae think anyone other than the immediate members of the MacLaren family knew of it."

"You have an idea who took Royce?" she asked once they reach the kitchen again.

Garrick began pulling her toward the turret stairs. "Aye. Some of the boys have been playing pranks on Royce. They may be responsible."

"Why would they do something so dreadful to their liege lord's son?"

"Perchance 'tis jealousy," Garrick answered. They reached the floor with a hidden passageway to the strand below. "If such is the case, 'twill not go well once the boy's parents are confronted by Laird Dristan."

Garrick stood in front of what appeared to be a solid stone wall. His fingers reaching beneath the facade, he felt the hidden latch and, with a click, released the mechanism and swung open a doorway.

"My word!" Coira gasped.

"'Tis a passageway that leads down to the beach," Garrick answered, once more taking another torch to light their way. "It has been used by the MacLarens for as long as I can remember tae escape in the event of a siege. Ye must keep it a secret."

"Of course, I will, Garrick, but if the boys have hidden Royce somewhere in this cave, then 'tis not much of a secret anymore."

"Ye may be right on that account, my love." He placed a quick kiss upon her lips. "Watch yer footing. The steps may get slippery."

With the hidden doorway closing behind them, they were plunged into darkness in the damp passageway. Their only light flickered as they descended the man-made steps. The smell of mildew assaulted their senses but 'twas far preferable than the odors they encountered in Berwyck's dungeons.

'Twere no other options than going downward, so Garrick was certain they could not miss Royce as they made their way lower. He had just about given up hope when they came to a landing more than half way down. The torch flooded the area. Royce, bound and gagged with tears streaming down his face, sat on a small stool next to a wooden chest.

Relief that they had found the lad flooded through Garrick while Coira rushed to her nephew and began to untie the boy.

She ran her hands over his face looking for injuries then she pulled him into her arms when the boy began to cry.

"Thank God we have found you, Royce," she cooed.

"They were so mean to me, Aunt Coira." Royce wrapped his arms around her.

Garrick came to kneel next to them. "Are ye all

right, Royce" he asked and suddenly found his arms filled with the lad.

"I knew you would be the one to find me, Garrick," Royce said and smiled broadly as Garrick released him.

"As long as ye are unharmed, that is all that matters." Garrick helped Coira to her feet. "We may as well head to the strand. 'Twill be far easier than climbing back up all those stairs."

Coira took Royce's hand and Garrick led the rest of the way till they saw a small measure of daylight. The entrance to the cave was hidden by vines and shrubbery but they easily exited the tunnel to encounter what was left of the day.

As they began making their way along the strand toward the castle, some of the knights searching the area saw the three of them and a cheer rang out. The knights' horses quickly lessened the distance and soon they were all riding back to the keep.

Dristan and Amiria must have been alerted that their son had been found for they were waiting in the stable yard. Amiria gushed over Royce, smothering him with kisses before the lad asked her to stop. Dristan came to the lad and lifted him up into his arms in a fierce hug. With Royce perched on his hip, he turned to Garrick and bowed, mouthing *thank you*.

Garrick gave him a courtly bow in return before Dristan and Amiria left to take their son inside. The implications of what he had done for his liege lord were momentarily lost on him, for Coira rushed to his side, winding her arms around his neck and pulling his head down.

Her lips met his and Garrick forgot everything else than showing this beautiful lady how much she meant to him.

CHAPTER 14

Moira stood once more on the parapet staring off to the distant horizon. After a good night's rest following a celebration that Berwyck's heir had been found, the morning breeze was refreshing, with a lingering hint of the salty ocean. She had found her home here among her cousin's people and felt accepted amongst them.

Morgan had sought her out last eve and, after much arguing on his part, she at last convinced the man that her feelings for Garrick would not change. If Dristan would not give his consent that they marry, she would go to a nunnery, for she would not marry another. She prayed such would not be the outcome. Her cousin loved her too much to condemn her to the fate of being a nun without a vocation.

She thought of the last time she had stood here in this exact place, her brother a ghostly vision that put her soul at ease, knowing he would watch over her. Her breath hitched. She knew he was somehow near even though she could not physically see him. Oh, how she missed him.

The turret door creaked open and none other the man of her dreams stepped through the portal with an endearing smile etched across his face.

He pulled on the strap around his shoulder and brought a lute forward. Placing his fingers on the strings he began to play an old Scottish melody that Coira remembered from her youth. He strode forward, still playing, and a look of delighted surprise swept across her face. She had no idea he knew how to play the instrument as he began serenading her.

Garrick brightened her day with the smile he bestowed upon her as he began to draw near. When he reached her side, she returned his smile with one of her own. "I see you are a man of many talents."

"I would fill all the rest of yer days with music if ye would give me the opportunity," he replied. Finishing the last few chords, he took the lute and set it up against the wall.

Before she could answer him, he took a hold of her arm and pulled her inside his embrace. Fire rushed throughout her body. She watched in fascination when his pulse quickened at the base of his neck. "Tell me ye feel what is between us? Tell me how, when we touch, ye know inside yer heart we are supposed tae be together. We are like two halves that have become whole, Coira. I knew this the instant I saw ye on the lists that day. Did ye feel the same way, too?"

Coira nodded. "I will not lie and say I did not feel some connection between us. I cannot even explain how I wandered onto the lists. I have no recollection of walking in your direction. I only knew I had somehow unknowingly moved forward to get closer to one knight in particular. That knight was you... even though I had no idea who you were." She watched him attempt to get control of himself and then she stepped closer.

Her arms went around his waist, and he reached up to brush away the tears falling gently down her cheeks. "And what of our kisses, lassie? Have ye thought about those too?" Garrick inquired.

A gasp escaped her, knowing Garrick had also thought about those kisses they had shared. He took hold of her face and watched her closely whilst awaiting her answer.

"I have dreamed of your kisses, Garrick. You honored me with my first kiss, and I want you to be the one who gives me my last," she replied, smiling and beginning to blush.

He placed a kiss upon her forehead before once more holding her close. "I will have ye know that I have spoken tae Fira and told her I love another. She willnae be bothering us anymore."

"You were kind to her when you told her your affections went to another?" Coira asked softly.

"Aye. As kind as I could be. She wasnae pleased but I believe she understood. In truth, I have no idea why she thought I cared for her as more than just a friend. I swear I never encouraged her," Garrick muttered.

"Let us not speak more of her. I believe you owe me a kiss," Coira urged with a laugh.

"Do I now?" he teased, as he tilted her chin so she had no choice but to look up into his mesmerizing eyes.

"Aye, you do, Garrick of Clan MacLaren," she said happily. "I meant it when I told Dristan I loved you."

"As I love you, my sweet lass," Garrick murmured, caressing her cheek.

Coira's heart rejoiced at his reply before he leaned down to brush his lips against hers. His moan of pleasure removed any further fears that he did not love her as she did him. He deepened their kiss and wound his arms around Coira, pulling her closer. She kissed him back just as fiercely, as though she never wished to let him go.

The *chink chink* of chainmail from a nearby knight keeping guard as he paced the battlement wall brought them back to their senses. Garrick released Coira and tucked a stray lock of hair behind her ear. He kissed her forehead whilst she composed herself and ensured she appeared presentable.

"What do we do now?" she asked in a breathy whisper, her lips most likely rosy red from his kisses.

"I am sure 'twill come tae us," he replied, sounding full of hope.

Garrick held out his hand to her, and she clasped her fingers within his. He lifted her hand to his lips before tucking her trembling limb in the crook of his arm. Grabbing his lute, he guided her towards the turret door. She nudged herself closer to his side, and her heart soared, knowing she had somehow captured her piper's heart.

EPILOGUE

Berwyck's Great Hall
One Fortnight Later

Garrick entered the great hall and a loud cheer roared throughout the crowded room.

Was it only last eve that his liege lord had met him in his hall asking Garrick to accompany him to the outer bailey? As they made their way outside, Laird Dristan began explaining he had a gift to bestow upon Garrick for saving his son. But Garrick never expected to see what was before him.

Coira stood smiling next to a pair of fully kitted out war horses. A servant held chainmail and helmet and a full array of knightly weapons were nearby. For him? Surely not. He could afford to maintain his own horse, but not two more, and expensive war horses at that.

He turned his attention from the horses in time to see Laird Dristan exchange a smile with Coira. He told all who were listening that his ward's husband would have no problem keeping her in the style to which she was accustomed. Coira came to him, holding out her hand. He gladly took it, placing a kiss upon her knuckles. Her eyes shone like the brightest of stars.

Their moment was brief and interrupted when Laird Dristan ordered Garrick to follow a servant to his new quarters in the family wing. He was to bathe, dress, and spend the night in prayer in the chapel. Tomorrow he would be knighted, an honor he had earned for the training he had done over the past several months along for his bravery and cleverness in finding Dristan's son.

His gaze swept the room until his eyes landed on the lady of his choice. Now that he was in truth a knight of the realm and his laird's blessing had been given, Garrick felt worthy enough to wed the fair Coira.

He watched as Royce began playing with the very same boys that had been tormenting him. After a substantial punishment from their parents that befitted their young age, the boys had been forgiven and Garrick hoped there would be peace between the lads from now on. Friendships that sometimes lasted a lifetime could begin after such a misunderstanding.

There was no further time to contemplate young

Royce. Not when Coira rushed up to him and grasped his hand. He lifted hers to his lips. "Sir Garrick, you are looking particularly handsome today," she whispered, pulling him to an alcove where they would not be seen.

"And ye are looking lovely today as well, my lady," he declared, before kissing her lips. But he did not linger longer than necessary and brought her once more forward so they were seen. "Dinnae look so disappointed, lassie. I willnae have my laird declaring I am unfit to wed ye now that he has given his blessing."

"We can talk about our wedding another day, Garrick. Today belongs to you," Coira murmured as she once more took his hand.

"I never thought tae have earned myself the honor of being one of Laird Dristan's guardsmen," Garrick said quietly.

She patted his arm. "You have earned the right to stand with them, my love. Never forget how hard you have been training. You have more than proved your worth, not only to be called a knight amongst them, but also to be my husband."

He looked down upon her whilst she smiled brightly upon him. "Ye shall not regret that we wed?" he asked, momentarily uncertain about her feelings for him. He ran his finger down her cheek before she took his hand and placed a kiss inside his palm.

"We belong together, Garrick of Clan MacLaren, whether you are a knight or the clan's piper. We shall have many happy years ahead of us and today is only the beginning. Let us dance!" she proclaimed with a laugh.

He leaned down and placed another quick kiss upon her lips before she left his side to join in the celebration. He lovingly watched her as she joined the women in a lively dance. When the vague image of her brother briefly revealed himself to Garrick, the ghost nodded his approval before he once more disappeared.

Garrick smiled in relief, but today was not the day to ponder what the future may hold. As long as Coira was happy to be the piper's lady, Garrick would do all within his power to ensure she never regretted her decision to love him.

'Twas a good beginning. He was content.

~

Sherry Ewing needs your help!

BOOK REVIEWS HELP readers to find books, and authors to find readers. Please consider writing a review for ***The Piper's Lady***, even a couple of sentences telling people what you liked (or didn't like) about the stories. Reviews can be posted on BookBub, Goodreads, and on most eRetailers websites. For links to this book on those sites, see Sherry's website at https://sherryewing.com/books/the-pipers-lady/

Sherry appreciates the time you take to write your reviews and, yes, she reads them all! Thank you for purchasing a copy of *The Piper's Lady*. Sherry hopes you've enjoyed Garrick and Coira's journey to finding love!

AUTHOR NOTES

Dearest Reader:

Thank you so much for purchasing this extended edition of *The Piper's Lady*. I hope you enjoyed Garrick and Coira's journey to finding love! How about a little lesson with history?

I know when most people think of bagpipes, we think of the Scottish Highlands and gorgeous men in kilts. But did you know that my research had me learning that the possible ancient origins of the bagpipe dates back to 1000 BC? Considering the title of this novella, it was important for me to ensure that some form of bagpipe existed in twelfth-century England.

As an example, take a look at this sculpture of a medieval bagpiper at Monastery of Santes Creus, Catalonia, Spain, constructed between 1174 and 1225. It's not what we envision today, but shows that some form of a reed pipe with a bladder was used during this period in time.

Château d'Usson was used at the beginning of The Piper's Lady for the location of where Morgan at last found Coira and her grandfather. "The castle dates from the 11th century (perhaps earlier) and during the Cathar period marked the eastern boundary of the territories of the Counts of Foix. In the 12th century, this was the capital of the Donézan region. Before the *défilé* was cut through the mountains to link Quillan to Axat, this was an inaccessible outpost providing succour for faidits and other persecuted Cathars. The Cathar bishop of Toulouse Guilhabert de Castres is known to have taken refuge here. Towards the end of the wars against the Cathars, this was one of their last sanctuaries, providing support for Montségur. The seigneurs of Usson, Bernard

d'Alion, lord of the Château de Montaillou, and his brother Arnaud d'Usson sent arms and supplies to their besieged comrades there. On 15 March 1244, the day before 225 Cathar *parfaits* were burned alive at Montségur, four other *parfaits* left the castle there for Usson, where the Cathar treasure had been evacuated a few months earlier. This mystery has fed a number of theories about the equally mysterious treasure supposedly found at Rennes-le-Château in the 19th century." (reference:
https://en.wikipedia.org/wiki/Château_d%27Usson)

As in my other medieval/time travel series, Berwyck Castle was actually located at Berwick-Upon-Tweed and I changed the name to suit the purposes of my stories. I hope you've been enjoying the return to my castle on the borders of Scotland and England!

Special thanks to Caroline Warfield and Jude Knight for taking time to beta read this extended edition. I also offer my thanks to Jude as my editor who continues to give my work that extra bit of life to truly make it shine. Thank you, ladies.

Thank you to the ladies on my review team! I appreciate your continued support by reading advance reader copies of my books and getting reviews up so other readers can find my work.

And, of course, my sincere thanks to you, my dearest reader, for continuing to read the stories I put out for your reading enjoyment. You are the reason why I write. I couldn't do this without you.

Until the next time, I look forward to reading your posts on social media. Be good to one another and stay safe!

With much love,
Sherry Ewing

OTHER BOOKS BY SHERRY EWING

Medieval & Time Travel Series

To Love A Scottish Laird: De Wolfe Pack Connected World

Sometimes you really can fall in love at first sight…

To Love An English Knight: De Wolfe Pack Connected World

Can a chance encounter lead to love?

If My Heart Could See You: The MacLarens, A Medieval Romance (Book One)

When you're enemies, does love have a fighting chance?

For All of Ever: The Knights of Berwyck, A Quest Through Time (Book One)

Sometimes to find your future, you must look to the past…

Only For You: The Knights of Berwyck, A Quest Through Time (Book Two)

Sometimes it's hard to remember that true love conquers all, only after the battle is over…

Hearts Across Time: The Knights of Berwyck (Books One & Two)

Sometimes all you need is to just believe… Hearts Across Time is a special edition box set that combines Katherine and Riorden's stories together from *For All of Ever* and *Only For You.*

A Knight To Call My Own: The MacLarens, A Medieval Romance (Book Two)

When your heart is broken, is love still worth the risk?

To Follow My Heart: The Knights of Berwyck, A Quest Through Time (Book Three)

Love is a leap. Sometimes you need to jump…

The Piper's Lady: The MacLarens, A Medieval Romance (Book Three)

True love binds them. Deceit divides them. Will they choose love?

Love Will Find You: The Knights of Berwyck, A Quest Through Time (Book Four)

Sometimes a moment is all we have…

One Last Kiss: The Knights of Berwyck, A Quest Through Time (Book Five)

Sometimes it takes a miracle to find your heart's desire…

Regency

A Kiss For Charity: A de Courtenay Novella (Book One)

Love heals all wounds but will their pride keep them apart?

The Earl Takes A Wife: A de Courtenay Novella (Book Two)

It began with a memory, etched in the heart.

Nothing But Time: A Family of Worth (Book One)

They will risk everything for their forbidden love...

One Moment In Time: A Family of Worth (Book Two)

One moment in time may be enough, if it lasts forever...

Under the Mistletoe

A new suitor seeks her hand. An old flame holds her heart. Which one will she meet under the kissing bough?

A Second Chance At Love in

Fire & Frost: A Bluestocking Belles Collection

Can the bittersweet frost of lost love be rekindled into a burning flame?

You can find out more about Sherry's work on her website at www.SherryEwing.com and at online retailers.

SOCIAL MEDIA

Website: www.SherryEwing.com
Email: Sherry@SherryEwing.com
Bluestocking Belles: www.bluestockingbelles.net/
Amazon Author Page: http://amzn.to/1TrWtoy
Bookbub: www.bookbub.com/authors/sherry-ewing
Facebook: www.Facebook.com/SherryEwingAuthor
Goodreads: www.Goodreads.com/author/show/8382315.Sherry_Ewing
Instagram: https://instagram.com/sherry.ewing
Pinterest: www.Pinterest.com/SherryLEwing
Tumblr: https://sherryewing.tumblr.com
Twitter: www.Twitter.com/Sherry_Ewing
YouTube: http://www.youtube.com/SherryEwingauthor

Sign Me Up!

Newsletter: http://bit.ly/2vGrqQM
Facebook Street Team: www.facebook.com/groups/799623313455472/
Facebook Official Fan page: https://www.facebook.com/groups/356905935241836/

ABOUT SHERRY EWING

Sherry Ewing picked up her first historical romance when she was a teenager and has been hooked ever since. A bestselling author, she writes historical and time travel romances to awaken the soul one heart at a time. When not writing, she can be found in the San Francisco area at her day job as an Information Technology Specialist.

Learn more about Sherry at:
Website: www.SherryEwing.com
Email: Sherry@SherryEwing.com

Printed in Great Britain
by Amazon

53021678R00076